THE FIRES AT
FITCH'S FOLLY

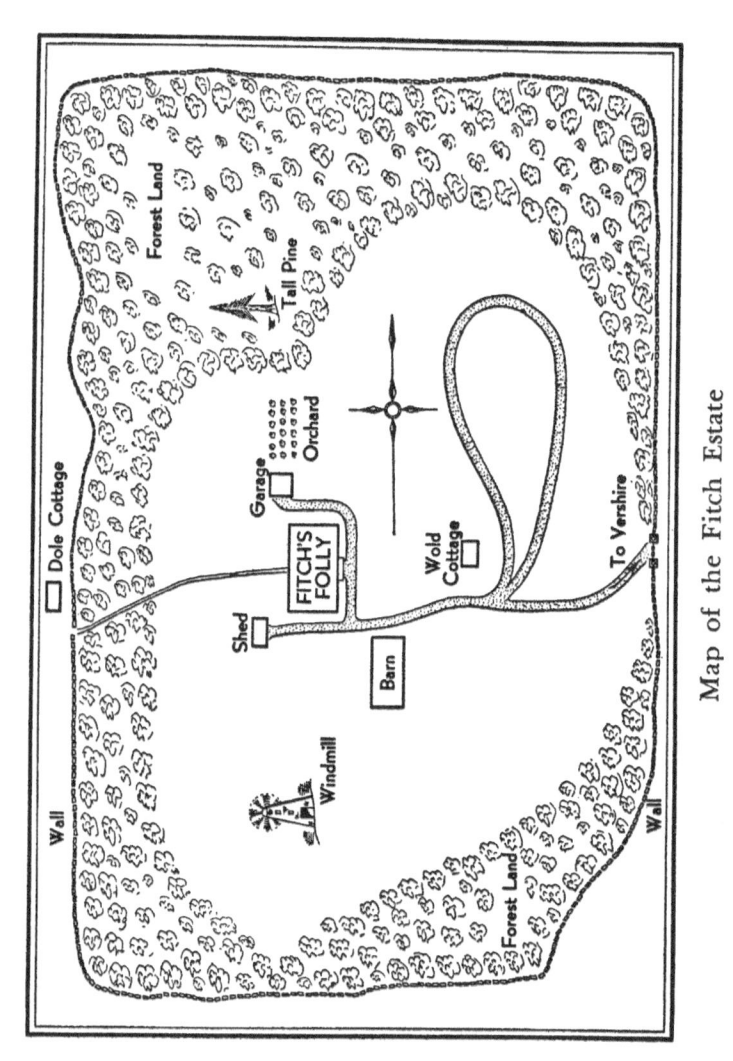

Map of the Fitch Estate

THE FIRES AT FITCH'S FOLLY

Kenneth Whipple

COACHWHIP PUBLICATIONS

GREENVILLE, OHIO

The Fires at Fitch's Folly, by Kenneth Whipple
© 2017 Coachwhip Publications

Published 1935
No claims made on public domain material.
Cover image: Fire © Magnilion

CoachwhipBooks.com

ISBN 1-61646-420-8
ISBN-13 978-1-61646-420-2

BARNBURNER

KENNETH WHIPPLE AND *THE FIRES AT FITCH'S FOLLY*

CURTIS EVANS

I. Kenneth Whipple (1894-1974)

Kenneth Duane Whipple's New England ancestors—a body which included William Whipple, a signer of the Declaration of Independence as a representative from New Hampshire—might have been scandalized had they lived to see their twentieth-century relation moonlighting as a crime writer, particularly as his crime writing sustained itself on the dark and bloody soil of the pulps. A ninth-generation New Englander on the Whipple side, whose original Puritan immigrant ancestor, Matthew Whipple, in the late 1630s migrated to the recently founded Ipswich, Massachusetts from Bocking, Essex (separated by a road from Braintree, Essex, whence came another Puritan, Henry Adams, founder of the American Adams family dynasty), Kenneth Whipple lived most of his life in rural eastern New Hampshire, across the Connecticut River from Vermont. In the 1930s he published "The Gray Death," a long novella written in the heedless and headlong style of Edgar Wallace shockers, which appeared only in pulp form, in *Complete Detective Novel Magazine* (1934), as well as a trio of crime novels, the first two of which—the topographically titled *The Murders at Loon Lake* (1933) and *The Killings in Carter's Cave* (1934)—had their origins in the pulps, while the last, *The Fires at Fitch's Folly* (1935), a fine essay in foreboding mystery told in the suspenseful manner of bestselling American author Mary Roberts Rinehart (who summered in Bar Harbor,

KENNETH WHIPPLE

Author of "The Fires at Fitch's Folly"

Kenneth Whipple comes of old New England stock. His ancestors came over soon after the Mayflower, and have lived in New England most of their lives. He was born in North Charlestown, N. H., in 1894. He early joined the staff of the *Claremont Daily Eagle,* with which he is still connected. In March, 1918, he went to Washington to work in the Bureau of War Risk Insurance, but says that his military service never took him more than thirty miles from home.

"My first short story," he says, "was sold in 1921 to *Detective Story Magazine.* For a time I tried other forms of fiction, and sold some of them, too, but as I found the detective and mystery stuff seemed to sell more readily than the other, I gradually concentrated on that. Since that date I have written and sold nearly $5000 worth of fiction, and have written and *not* sold at least as much more. 'The Fires at Fitch's Folly' is my fourth complete detective novel. Being a newspaper man, I probably need not state that my writing is done in spare time."

Maine), was only "pulped," so to speak, after its publication as a novel. Herein *The Fires at Fitch's Folly* sees print again, for the first time in over eighty years.

Kenneth Duane Whipple was born in the Connecticut River valley village of North Charlestown, New Hampshire on April 11, 1894, the son of Charles Eugene Whipple, a carpenter and incorrigible patentee (among other things he patented a "new and improved crank-motion" in 1875 and a folding chair design in 1906), upon whom Kenneth seems to have partially based a character in "The Gray Death," and his wife Bessie Mabelle Breed. As a high schooler in the early 1910s, young Whipple, reflecting his father's skill with his hands, operated a linotype (a machine used to set type for newspapers) at the *Daily Eagle*, a newspaper in the neighboring town of Claremont. Barring a stint in service during and immediately after the U. S. participation in the First World War, when he held a desk job in Washington, D. C. at the Bureau of War Risk Insurance, the predecessor of the Veterans Administration (Whipple would later draw on this locale in "The Gray Death"), the brown-haired, green-eyed Whipple would work for the *Eagle* for most of the rest of his life, rising to the position of editor before his retirement in the 1960s.

With the publication of "The Purple Brick" in *Detective Story Magazine* on April 23, 1921, not long after he left Washington and returned to Claremont (and less than two weeks after his twenty-seventh birthday), Whipple commenced a fifteen-year career as a crime fiction writer. In addition to his three novels and single novella, all of which appeared in the pulps between 1930 and 1936, Whipple published, mostly in *Detective Story Magazine*, at least 36 pulp crime fiction short stories, all but one of them during the Roaring Twenties. These included such titles as "Drawn Shades," "The Deadly Female," "Thunder of Doom," "Tainted" and "Pursued" (the latter pair his only publications in the greatest pulp of them all, *Black Mask*). Whipple later estimated that during these years he sold nearly $5000 worth of fiction to the pulps (nearly $90,000 today)—a not insignificant supplement to his newspaper work.

In the 1930s, Whipple, following the enticing examples of such hard-boiled pulp writers as Dashiell Hammett and Raoul Whitfield, turned away from writing short fiction in favor of novels, but he found that pressing work and family obligations made it hard for him to continue his fiction writing. Whipple, who had married Edna Sarah Kemp in 1917 and with her fathered three children, tellingly dedicated *The Fires at Fitch's Folly*, which was published by Thomas Y. Crowell in 1935, *TO ALL MY FRIENDS—In spite of whom this story was finished.* He also commented that, "Being a newspaper man, I probably need not state that my writing is done in spare time." *Folly*'s appearance in *Mystery Novels Magazine* the next year seems to have marked Whipple's retirement, at the relatively youthful age of 42, as an author of crime fiction.

If such was indeed the case, *The Fires at Fitch's Folly* made an enticing swan song, Isaac Anderson in the *New York Times Book Review* declaring that the novel "has suspense and thrills in plentiful measure" and another reviewer (this one in the *Paris News*—not of Paris, France, but rather Paris, Texas) affirming that it "makes agreeably exciting and baffling reading."

II. *The Fires at Fitch's Folly* (1935)

> *You who have followed this chronicle thus far may feel, perhaps justifiably, that you are not being treated fairly in the matter of clues. In these pages you will fail to find the detailed diagram, the cigarette butt, the mudstain, the fingerprint, the telltale time schedule, the trickily phrased interrogation with its revelatory replies, and all the other customary paraphernalia of detection.*
>
> *For these omissions, my apologies. They cannot be helped. I am merely telling the tale of those July days as their dread panorama unrolled itself before my own eyes from ominous morning to fear-filled night.*

The Fires at Fitch's Folly is set during a wicked hot July in northern New England, in the fictional town of Vershire (an obvious amalgam of Vermont and New Hampshire), cite of Fitch's Folly, the "outlandish"—at least "to the frugal residents of the New England valley town"—summer estate of elderly and eccentric Peter Fitch, an Albany, New York millionaire. Fitch's family and servitors at his Folly consist of his overshadowed middle-aged son, Guy, Guy's wife, Martha, and the couple's "vivid and vivacious" Vassar graduate daughter, Patricia ("Patty"); his strident, "horse-faced" spouse, Nellie, and Nellie's faded widowed sister, Mrs. Alice Lodge; his "dumbly devoted" German butler and valet, Karl Litzler; his stolid gardener, George Wold, George's eldritch wife, Margery and their gangling, "half-wit" son, Wentworth ("Wenty"); his two daily domestics, Della Dole and Mary Anderson; and his recently acquired chauffeur, Bill Perley, the narrator of the novel and admiring "Watson" to the keen-minded Vershire Chief of Police, Larry Frost, who, in a startling coincidence, was Bill's second in command during the Great War (see below). Also figuring in the crowded though clearly written story are County Solicitor Gene Hawkins; medical referee Dr. Henry Reefer; assorted law enforcement underlings (Jim Forbes, John Duncan, Zenas Williams, and Jesse Peabody); Mr. Brown and Mr. Robinson, a couple of suspicious characters staying at the local inn; and a trio of summer guests at Fitch's Folly: Patty Fitch's handsome beau, Gilbert; her charming old college girlfriend, Ruth Vale; and an enigmatic visitor by the name of Dinwiddie. And let's not by any means forget the neighborhood's passing tramp!

The novel's aforementioned narrator, Bill Perley, is a much put-upon individual indeed. A sufferer from pyrophobia on account of his having nearly been consumed in the childhood conflagration that killed his parents, Bill was drummed out of the army during the Great War after he, an infantry captain, fled "in stark terror to the rear" of the lines upon his "initial encounter with the German *flammenwerfers.*" Moreover, he later served jail time for, as the saying goes, a crime he didn't commit. (To top it off he was framed for the crime by a friend.) Down on his luck and with the wolf at his door (a state of affairs with which, no doubt, many Depression-era readers could identify), Bill ended up as Peter Fitch's chauffeur, a position he was glad to get at the time, though the mere thought of that menial status obviously mortifies him.

Bill thus was on hand to later tell the tale when, on the evening of the Third of July, the barn at Fitch's Folly went up in smoke. After the fire was finally put out, police made a gruesome discovery: a charred skeleton—with a bullet hole in its skull! As reminiscently related by Bill, this was the first of several fearsome fires—and several fiendish murders—to strike Fitch's Folly, until the dauntless Police Chief Frost finally iced an insidious and crafty killer.

Despite having received good reviews upon its publication in 1935, *The Fires at Fitch's Folly* for more than eight decades languished out-of-print and forgotten, with, before now, one exception of which I am aware: the ever-aware crime writer Bill Pronzini, who allows the novel to play a part in the resolution of his fine 2009 Nameless detective novel, *Schemers*. After finishing *The Fires at Fitch's Folly*, fans of *Fires* should check out *Schemers*, if they have not read it already.

THE FIRES AT
FITCH'S FOLLY

To All My Friends
In spite of whom this story was finally finished

CHAPTER I
STAGE SETTING

Old Peter Fitch, my employer, was a millionaire several times over—was, in fact, rated as one of the richest men in Albany. He had made his money in steel in the early days of the industry. Now, at seventy, still incredibly spry and active, he lived in comparative seclusion, dividing his time between his Albany mansion, his son Guy's estate on Long Island, and his own summer home—Fitch's Folly—at Vershire in northern New England.

Incredible legends had grown up about him—that he was a miser, that he was a gold hoarder, that he still had the first silver dollar he ever earned, that he never trusted a penny of his fortune to a bank.

These tales, while categorically false, were not without some foundation in fact. Though prone to gratify every whim regardless of cost, to other members of his family he was parsimonious to a fault. He had turned in a huge amount of gold at the first Federal anti-hoarding order, though he was reputed to have plenty more in his safe; and if he had any souvenir silver dollars, I have never seen them. Also, although he was on the directorate of a half dozen financial institutions, he invariably carried an inordinately large amount of cash on his person and kept many times that sum on the premises.

By turns he was kindly, sarcastic, unbearably crotchety, and almost unbelievably eccentric. Despite the fact that his son Guy was nearing his fiftieth birthday and had a daughter just out of Vassar, Peter Fitch was still the head of the family and ruled his tribe with a rod of iron. He was more friendly, in fact, with his employees than with his relatives. Certainly he was with me.

It would be well, perhaps, to sketch briefly the circumstances under which I became his chauffeur. Temporarily jobless and completely discouraged, I had been hitch-hiking from New York to Albany that spring with the faint hope of getting a job from an old war buddy who had inherited a factory and a half million or so. And on this expedition, a few miles north of Kingston, I had chanced to be an eye-witness of a head-on collision and motor holocaust in which old Peter's chauffeur, trapped in his blazing limousine, had lost his life.

Peter Fitch himself had been miraculously spared, having left the car a moment earlier to pluck a spray of spring flowers from the embankment above the highway. Somehow we had fallen into conversation as we stood watching the futile efforts of the rescuers. A half hour later, in a new limousine which had appeared startlingly from nowhere, I was driving my new boss on toward Albany.

"Think I'm crazy, hiring you like this—eh?" he cackled en route, twitching my sleeve with his skinny hand. "That's the way I do things— snap judgment! That's the way I've done things all my life! That's the way I've made money! I'll check up on you later, of course—but I'm not wrong! I know I'm not wrong! I'm never wrong!"

And in this off-hand fashion I became chauffeur for Peter Fitch. Save for that crash high above the banks of the Hudson, I would never have become entangled in the startling series of events which were to focus the eyes of the entire nation on Fitch's Folly before the dread summer had run its course.

I had never seen Peter Fitch before the day I entered his employ, though naturally I had read of him in the public prints. He was a wizened, shrunken little man whose head, bristling with an untidy mop of snow-white hair, came scarcely to my shoulder. The skin of his face was leathery, and his fingers were little better than skinny claws. But for all his age, there was still about him a sort of electric vitality which seemed fairly to radiate from his sparse and shrunken frame.

The feature which had most deeply impressed me on the day of the car fire, however, had been his extraordinary eyes. Of an opaque, slaty blue-gray, with a skein of fine wrinkles at the corners, they had mirrored uncannily the look I felt must be in my own—a compound of fascination and fear, with an added tinge of something bordering on exultation.

For I may as well confess at the outset my own fear of fire. It is more than a fear—it is a genuine phobia, with doubtless some lengthy scientific name. It is, intensified a hundredfold, the instinctive, unreasoning dread of the burned child.

Whether the fact that I was literally a burned child is entirely responsible, I do not know. It seems sometimes that there must have been also some pre-natal proclivity, some hereditary influence. I only know that since that bitter winter's night when, at the age of four, I was brought with clothing ablaze from the conflagration in which both my parents perished, my nightmares have invariably been of blistering sheets of flame swirling about me while I lie helpless and paralyzed.

This fear, until recently, has never for an instant left me. Waking and sleeping, I have died literally scores of deaths in torment. Indeed, as a captain of infantry two decades later, my initial encounter with the German *flammenwerfers*—the terrible flame-throwers of the World War—had sent me cringing in stark terror to the rear, there to face a court-martial which stripped me of my rank and sent me home in disgrace.

I make this admission and this apology freely, for I have no intention and no desire to pose as the hero of this chronicle. The credit, such as it is, goes to Larry Frost, chief of the Vershire police department, for his herculean labors in unraveling the tangled skein of hideous happenings which made the summer of 193– at Fitch's Folly an unforgettable nightmare.

Old Peter, as I have said, seemingly shared my fire phobia—indeed, I always attributed the impulse on which he had hired me to the fact that we were in a sense kindred spirits. By a curious coincidence, I later learned, he too had had a narrow escape from death by fire in his youth, having been one of the few survivors of a tragic dormitory blaze which is still a dark blot on the annals of one of our oldest colleges.

At the outset I believed him slightly unbalanced on the subject, though, before the summer had sped, a day was to come when I no longer held with that belief. He belabored the topic interminably on many of our trips together—for old Peter, I soon discovered, was a democratic soul and characteristically disdained the rear seat save on state occasions.

"It's all a plot, Bill—all these fires!" he once told me earnestly. "You're afraid of them too—aren't you, Bill? Remember the day my old car burned?"

I shuddered involuntarily, feeling my lips and cheeks stiffen.

"Why do you think it's a plot, sir?" I asked.

Old Peter's slaty eyes glinted.

"I know it's a plot!" he shrilled. "They're after my money—the whole lot of 'em—but I'll fool 'em yet! They'll have to get up pretty early in the morning to catch Peter Fitch!"

Then, two weeks later, we were at Vershire, and the stage was set for the tragic midsummer drama of Fitch's Folly.

There are many towns in which the name "Folly" has fastened itself upon some elaborate mansion built in the earlier days of its history by some dweller now dead and gone. In Vershire it was the Fitch estate, planned as a show place by old Herkimer Fitch, father of Peter, and erected at a cost which, a half century ago, had seemed outlandish to the frugal residents of the New England valley town.

Fitch's Folly sprawled across the entire top of a minor mountain, which thrust itself skyward just west of the town. Although the air line distance could have been little more than a mile, the winding highway which led up to it measured more than twice that distance. The slopes below were mainly virgin forest, and the estate, embracing, I believe, nearly two hundred acres, was completely surrounded by a thick stone wall broken only by a single pair of cast-iron gates affording entry by road and a smaller opening for a footpath leading in from the rear.

The house itself, facing eastward, overlooked the town and the valley below. It was of the ornate, rambling type in which architects of an earlier day delighted. It contained sixteen huge rooms, high-ceilinged and spacious, while the barn and stable which had once sheltered old Herkimer's string of racing horses was nearly as large. The house was topped by an octagonal cupola with a pointed roof and a huge gilt weathervane which had unquestionably been to its designer the *ne plus ultra* of ornamentation.

Beside the house and barns, there were all sorts of outbuildings—a gardener's cottage, a garage, a shed where the thrifty Herkimer once stored his winter's supply of wood, and other minor structures too numerous to mention.

Add to these a pergola, a sunken garden, a grape arbor, a windmill for pumping water with an auxiliary gasoline engine in the small shack beneath its straddling steel legs; picture a pair of cast-iron stags on the green slopes of the immense lawns; visualize more than a mile of gravel drives winding through the spacious grounds—and you will gain at least a fair idea of the estate dubbed (perhaps not without cause) "Fitch's Folly."

I have given so much space, in this perhaps too lengthy preamble, to the character of Peter Fitch and the description of his summer home, because of their vital integration in the insane and seemingly meaningless series of events which impended. I will now seek to sketch in the other members of the household—these more briefly, though their roles in some instances were scarcely minor ones.

Peter Fitch's wife, Nellie, a large-boned, horse-faced woman with protuberant eyes and a strident voice, merits unquestionably the head of the list. Her sister, Mrs. Alice Lodge, was almost her exact antithesis—quiet, subdued, ladylike, a faded, spinsterish widow whom one could never imagine having been married.

Nellie Fitch, I quickly learned, had little use for her sister, and lost no opportunity to remind her that she was a member of the household only through old Peter's sufferance—which, incidentally, happened to be strictly true. The mutual antipathy—for it was mutual —puzzled me for some time before I learned that the relationship was only that of half-sisters.

Guy Fitch, the son, I did not particularly like—a tall, hard, semibald individual with a long, pointed red face and a neck like a turkey's. He was altogether too fond of issuing pointless orders in the absence of his father, though when old Peter was about he assumed an attitude of meek subservience which, whatever else it may have accomplished, failed completely to deceive the staff of servants.

His wife, Martha, was more likeable, though the blonde, chinadoll beauty which she had undeniably possessed in her youth had long since faded. Though devoted to her husband and for the most part as wax in his hands, she could and did, on occasion, stand up for her rights with surprising vigor.

Patricia, their daughter, was almost the sole redeeming feature of the Fitch line. Vivid and vivacious, with the unusual and irresistible

combination of dancing brown eyes and bobbed locks of almost
a platinum blonde, she was undeniably the life, such as it was, of
Fitch's Folly.

Two house guests had accompanied us from Albany to Vershire.
One was Gilbert Cooper, Patty's "boy friend"—a tanned, good-look-
ing ex-collegian lacking summer employment, for whom she had
wangled an invitation from her indulgent grandfather. The other was
Ruth Vale.

I cannot deny that I admired Miss Vale immensely from the outset—and, doubtless, showed it more than I realized. Though one of
Patty's former teachers, she had little of the schoolma'am about her.
She was, I judged, about thirty, with bright dark eyes and sleek hair
so dark that it looked, in some lights, almost blue-black. She was
wholly likeable and without airs or affectations of any sort. She had
come, at Patty's urgent invitation, to spend a week at Fitch's Folly
before going on to act as councilor in a girls' camp at Lake Winnepe-
saukee.

This completes the roster of the family and guests. Karl Litzler, a
stiff-backed German dumbly devoted to Peter Fitch, served as combination butler and valet, while Margery Wold, the gardener's wife,
was the only resident female domestic. Peter Fitch in this respect was
a stickler for simplicity, and Guy and Martha had learned that any
attempt to bring members of their own staff of servants to Fitch's
Folly was certain to provoke an outburst and an ultimatum.

And now a final word about the cottage of George Wold, the gardener, which came to play such a vital part in the fires at Fitch's Folly.

The cottage, located just over the brow of the eastward slope, was
invisible from the main floors of the mansion itself, though it could
be seen from the ornate cupola above. In it lived George the gardener, who with recruited amateur assistance from Vershire tended the
masses of flowers and kept the grounds in order. His wife acted as
cook and maid, and supervised the two non-resident domestics-by-
the-day—Della Dole and Mary Anderson—in their duties about the
house.

The Wolds had been with the Fitches for nearly thirty years, and
bade fair to continue until the end of their days. George was tall and
spare, with bowed shoulders and dull, deep-set eyes. Margery was

stocky and sturdy, with a tousled mane of coal-black hair and brilliant black eyes in which, some said, lurked more than a tinge of madness.

They had one son, Wentworth Wold—nicknamed, of course, Wenty. He was a gangling creature of nearly thirty, and was little better than a half-wit. Wenty was rarely seen outside the cottage save for the rambling excursions which he made at intervals through the woods of the estate. Suggestions that he be sent to the State hospital for the insane met with stiff opposition, both from his parents and from Peter Fitch himself, and admittedly Wenty had never shown symptoms of dangerous mania.

This, then, was the scene and these the characters on the night before the Fourth of July, when Fitch's Folly was visited by its first fire and its first tragedy.

CHAPTER II
CURTAIN!

The third of July, I recall clearly, was an ideal midsummer New England day, with no hint in its shimmering beauty of the blow about to befall. An overnight shower had made the air as clear as crystal, and the outlines of even the more distant mountains stood out distinctly against the lighter blue of the summer sky. The infrequent trains traversing the plain below were clearly visible, and even the infinitesimal dots of cars could be seen streaming along the highway paralleling the tracks.

I was not surprised at an order to meet a house guest arriving on the ten o'clock train; visitors at Fitch's Folly were by no means a rarity. I was surprised, however, when Guy, who had given the order, appeared at the garage to accompany me to Vershire. He appeared nervous and ill at ease, and the Adam's apple in his long neck moved up and down convulsively from time to time.

The guest, descending from the northbound train, proved to be a man about Guy's age and build, startlingly bald, with a furrowed face lit by a pair of deep-set, piercing eyes.

Guy hurried forward to meet him, and the pair went into a huddle by the corner of the station, their heads close together, for all the world like a couple of conspirators.

I had backed my car to the edge of the platform before Guy alighted. Now, relaxing, I watched them idly in the windshield mirror. The fantastic thought crossed my mind that Guy, weary of his father's domination, had imported a Gotham gunman to put old Peter on the spot.

How close to the truth my preposterous idea had been, I was not to learn until it was too late to matter.

I sprang out to open the door as the two at last approached. I had soon learned that Guy, unlike his father, was markedly punctilious regarding the behavior of menials.

To my surprise he paused to smile pleasantly, if nervously, at me before joining his guest in the rear seat of the limousine.

"Drive slowly up the Folly road, Bill," he ordered. "I want Dinwiddie here to get an eyeful of our view. He's new to this section of the country, and I want him to enjoy it."

The view, unfolding gradually as the car wound its way up the mountain side, was indeed well worth seeing. But before we were half-way to Fitch's Folly, I realized that neither Guy nor his companion was paying the slightest attention to the scenery. They were continuing, if one judged by glimpses caught in the windshield mirror, the discussion begun on the station platform, and the argument seemed to be growing acrimonious.

I wrenched my eyes determinedly away, but I could not completely close my ears. Tantalizing scraps of sentences reached me as one or the other of the disputants raised his voice to stress a point.

"—dangerous business, just the same."

"Dangerous? You're telling me! If I didn't feel sure—"

Unconsciously my foot relaxed on the throttle, and the voices sank to a murmur once more. But a moment later I caught:

—got to get away tonight. There's a chance—

"It's safe as a church, I tell you! He'll never—"

We rolled leisurely out of the encircling ring of virgin forest onto the gentler slopes of the broader driveway leading up to the house. Martha Fitch, Guy's wife, was standing on the steps as I halted the limousine beneath the porte-cochère.

More from curiosity than from any other motive, I took my time in shutting the door and resuming my seat behind the wheel.

"Dinwiddie," Guy said, still (it seemed) a little nervously, "I want you to meet Mrs. Fitch. Martha, this is the business friend from New York I told you I was expecting today. Have Karl show him to the room next to mine."

Guy's wife was voicing a formal greeting as, not daring to delay longer, I drove away toward the garage. It was obvious that, whatever had been his business relations with her husband, Dinwiddie was a complete stranger to Martha Fitch.

There were three cars at Fitch's Folly—Peter Fitch's big limousine, Guy's scarcely less pretentious sedan, and Patty's sports roadster. And though all members of the household (save Mrs. Lodge, who never touched a wheel) were expert drivers, I had found my post no sinecure.

Now, before I had scarcely garaged the limousine, Patty came dashing madly across the lawn, with Gilbert Cooper at her heels.

"Oh, Bill!"

"Yes, Miss Patty?"

"I'm awfully sorry—I meant to catch you before you left with Dad. Gilbert and I are both out of cigarettes, and something's gone haywire in my starter. Would you mind running us back downtown so we can get a couple of cartons? Dad's brand is simply poisonous, and Gramp never smokes anything but that lousy old pipe of his."

I acceded willingly, convinced that the trip was at least partially an excuse for a little refined petting en route. Before starting, however, I supplied both of my passengers from my own pack.

Patty, at times the soul of democracy, accepted with a gaminesque grin of appreciation that made me wonder anew how she could possibly be the child of Guy and Martha Fitch. It was rarely that one caught a glimpse, beneath the vivacious exterior, of the rock-ribbed ruthlessness which seemed to be her chief heritage from old Peter.

My notion of the prime purpose of the trip, however, proved erroneous. No petting of any sort, it developed, was in order. Instead, the entire journey was devoted to a serious, low-voiced conference, of which no word reached my undeniably curious ears.

They alighted in front of the drug store on the corner. Patty leaned in at the open window.

"Pick us up here in about a half hour," she said.

Touching my stiff-visored cap, I set the car in motion. Before I turned the corner, however, the ever-helpful windshield mirror had told me that they had not entered the drug store but had, after a momentary pause, crossed the street toward the court house.

Two blocks down the street I drew up in front of the Vershire police station, a small building standing well back from the curb— my favorite hangout downtown ever since I had discovered with gratification that Chief of Police Larry Frost was none other than my second in command at the time of the summary termination of my military service.

Larry, his lanky length sprawled in his swivel chair, greeted me cordially. He was tall and dark, with thick, almost curly black hair and eyes as brilliant—and as hard—as chips of black jade. His broad shoulders filled out his uniform snugly, though the general effect was slightly marred by a pair of huge feet which were uncomfortable in No. 12 shoes. He worked both himself and his men hard, and most criminals "in the know" had learned to give Vershire a wide berth.

"Hello, Bill!" he grinned. "How's everything up on the hill?"

"Quiet," I said, perching on the corner of the desk. "What's the latest down here?"

"Not much—except the fire last night. I suppose hell will be popping tonight and tomorrow, though, when the kids let loose with their fireworks—"

"What fire?" I interrupted. "I hadn't heard anything about it."

"Johnson's garage. Pretty well gutted, too. There's a theory it's a firebug, but I doubt it. I think old Johnson's trying to cash in on some of his insurance. I've got Jim Forbes working on it now."

"What time did all this happen?"

"Oh, about three o'clock this morning," yawned Larry. "You must have been dead to the world all right—you and that boss of yours both. He usually comes down every time we have a fire—can't keep away from them any more than a kid. He'll get killed some day, too, tearing down that mountain hell bent for election the way he does."

"He's more likely to get killed falling asleep in his chair with his pipe in his mouth," I said. "I understand he's started a couple of fires already that way. If he—"

I paused as an idea popped into my mind.

"At least, they were blamed on his pipe," I said slowly. "I wonder—say, maybe there's something to that fire phobia of his after all!"

"I guess Vershire wouldn't shed any tears if the whole place went up in smoke," commented Larry. "Perhaps you don't realize it, but your boss isn't exactly the most popular man in town. I can think of folks whose idea of fun would be to see old Fitch and the rest of the Folly gang sizzling—"

He broke off abruptly at sight of my face, which I knew from the familiar sensation of stiffness had gone dead white.

"Sorry, Bill," he said in a low tone. "I forgot!"

An awkward silence ensued. To Larry Frost, one night in the dug-out a week before my ordeal by fire, I had confided my secret fear. He alone of all my brother officers had known a little of the hidden terror which was my constant companion. And he alone, from our talks since I had come to Vershire, had learned of the six months' sentence I had since served for a crime I did not commit—the prison term that had shaken my grip on life and had left me with a dull hopelessness which made even my present menial status a matter of indifference.

Slowly the color crept back into my face. I even managed a crooked grin.

"That's O. K., Larry," I said a little shakily. "Forget it. What else is new?"

We chatted for perhaps another fifteen minutes before I departed. I drove around the block, renewed my own supply of cigarettes, and emerged from the drug store just as Patty and Gilbert were about to enter.

They both, I thought, seemed a little startled at sight of me. Patty, however, carried it off with her usual nonchalance.

"With you most any minute, Bill," she said. "Get the old crate to percolating."

Obediently I climbed in and started the engine, eyeing them meanwhile through the window to make certain they actually did buy cigarettes. At the time I was only mildly curious as to the nature of their other errand. It was doubtless the obvious mystery of Guy's guest that had made me abnormally inquisitive.

I pondered the problem idly for a time en route back to Fitch's Folly, then dismissed it from my thoughts. Garaging the limousine, I set to work on the starter of the roadster, which proved to need merely a thorough cleaning and readjusting of the armature and brushes.

It was rapidly approaching midday, and I was anxious to finish in time to clean up properly before the dinner hour. Margery Wold was abnormally fussy about the neatness of her kitchen, and I had no wish to incur her enmity.

As I lay supine and practically invisible beneath the car, the voice of Peter Fitch sounded outside the open window. His first words brought me semi-erect with such a start that I rapped my head smartly against the chassis.

"He's a firebug—mark my words!" the cracked voice was saying vehemently. "If we're all burned to death in our beds tonight—"

He broke off, apparently for some interruption which to me was inaudible. Squirming from beneath the car, I peered cautiously from the window.

Although I could see old Peter's face, in three-quarter profile, directed toward the hedge at the rear of the garage, I could not see to whom he was speaking. As I looked, he shook his claw-like finger warningly.

"I don't care what you say!" he cackled. "But you can put this in your pipe and smoke it—if anything happens, it won't be to old Peter Fitch! He's too wise a bird to let anybody put salt on his tail!"

Wheeling abruptly, he ambled away toward the house with his short, nimble-footed strides. I stared after him, more than a little perplexed. It was obvious, I told myself, that if some sort of a plot was afoot, it was not exactly news to Peter Fitch. And, despite his age and eccentricities, it did not occur to me to doubt that he was amply able to take care of himself.

Turning to my task, I had the satisfaction of getting the starter reassembled and functioning before one o'clock, the hour at which Karl and I ate our midday meal. Hurrying up the stairs to my sleeping quarters, a commodious room above the garage, I slipped off my overalls, cleaned the grime from my arms and hands, and made my way to the kitchen.

As I passed the open windows of the dining room I cast a curious glance within. The meal was over, but none had left the table. I saw Dinwiddie, his piercing eyes fixed on Peter Fitch, listening with attentive politeness to a discourse on the early morning fire at Vershire. I judged, from the few words I caught, that my employer was distributing with fine impartiality the blame for his failure to awaken or to be awakened.

Mary and Della, the two non-resident domestics, were laboring assiduously under the snapping black eyes of Margery as I entered the kitchen and seated myself at the table by the window. Karl had not yet appeared, and I found myself temporarily alone.

As I sat waiting to be served, I found myself eyeing the Fitch cook with recurrent curiosity. It had been several centuries since witchcraft was legally a crime in New England; the advance of civilization had set safeguards about such as Margery Wold. But I could not rid myself of the thought that some three hundred years earlier she would have provided an ideal subject for legalized burning.

I dropped my gaze hastily as she brought my plate. I did not believe in the "evil eye," in the sense that doubtless some of my ancestors had. But I could not deny that the dark flame of her glance possessed the power to make me distinctly uncomfortable.

Karl did not appear until I had nearly finished. He lowered himself wearily into the chair opposite me. His pale blue eyes held a worried look, and he ran his short, stumpy fingers perplexedly through his stiff, close-cropped hair.

"Always he iss getting worse," he said in a low tone.

"Who?"

"The master. Fires, fires, fires—always he talks of them. I haff been hearing him. If he iss so afraid, why does he not engage a guard?"

"He doesn't need one with you around, Karl," I said, half jokingly.

The stolid face of the butler-valet was lighted by a momentary gleam.

"I do my best," he said simply. "But the master—he iss getting old now, and maybe a little queer. Some day—"

He fell silent, shaking his head. I pushed back my plate and rose, leaving him still staring moodily at his plate.

I had never been able to understand Karl's doglike devotion to old Peter, which had always seemed too genuine to be a sycophantic pose. As for myself, I was perfectly willing to admit that excellent wages formed my sole tie with Fitch's Folly and its eccentric master.

The afternoon, as I recall, was comparatively uneventful. Patty and Gilbert went riding, using two of the saddle horses from the half dozen which still occupied the huge barn as a gesture by Peter Fitch in memory of Herkimer's racing string. Ruth Vale went riding also. She rode alone, however, and in a different direction, despite Patty's halfhearted urgings.

I did not see her when she returned, having gone to take Mrs. Lodge on one of her periodic visits to the Vershire Free Public Library. This was a sure aftermath, according to servants' gossip, of a blazing row with her half-sister or her brother-in-law. On such occasions Mrs. Lodge, very pale and dignified, invariably went to Vershire, brought home an armful of the lesser classics, shut herself in her room, and there read herself back to equanimity.

Patty and Gilbert I saw when they returned slowly just before supper. Both were astride Gilbert's mount, and Patty was leading her horse, which had stepped on a tilting stone and had gone dead lame.

A little of old Herkimer had cropped out in Guy, who was as fervent an equine enthusiast as his daughter. He assumed personal charge of treatment for Dolly's lameness, brushing aside the well-meant offer of aid made by Wenty, who appeared wraith-like from the dark recesses of the barn as they arrived.

It was Guy, also, who gave me orders to bring the car around at eight o'clock.

"Dinwiddie's train doesn't leave till eight-twenty," he said, his Adam's apple sliding up and down nervously. "But there mustn't be any chance of his missing it."

"Very well, sir," I said, touching my cap.

It was about 7:45 (as I recalled afterward) that from my window I saw Guy emerge from the side door of the house and hurry toward the barn. In one hand he carried a flat bottle, and in the other a roll of what appeared to be gauze.

"Still fussing around that damned horse," I said to myself.

The car was at the door promptly at eight. As it stopped Guy's guest hurried down the steps, looking anxiously about him. His face, in the half dusk of the dying day, looked queerly drawn and worried.

"Have you seen Mr. Fitch—Mr. Guy Fitch?" he asked in a cautious tone. "I have—er—just remembered something I wanted to tell him before I left."

"I think he's in the barn, sir," I said. "I'll stop if you wish to see."

The barn, a huge, gloomy structure, was perhaps fifty yards below the house and on the opposite side of the driveway. As I braked the car to a stop I glimpsed—or thought I did—a flickering gleam far in its dark recesses.

"I wouldn't be too long, sir," I warned. "It's hard to make speed safely down this winding road."

Dinwiddie, nodding, hurried into the barn. He was hurrying even faster when he emerged after a surprisingly short stay. Without a word he climbed into the rear seat, pulled the door shut behind him, and settled himself in silence in the far corner.

I set the car in motion without delay. While rail service up and down the valley was notoriously erratic, there was always a chance that a train might actually arrive on time. And I had no desire to incur Guy's wrath by permitting his guest to miss it.

Although the summit we had just quitted had barely lost the last thin rays of the setting sun, the valley below was already in semi-darkness. The inevitable firecrackers in the hands of impatient youngsters were sputtering intermittently in various sections of Vershire. Now and then a vagrant rocket, soaring aloft with a hiss, burst in a shower of stars, and some improvident soul was loosing a series of aerial bombs that reverberated from hill to hill like the rattle of musketry.

A deeper darkness had descended before we reached the railway station. We had nearly five minutes to spare—which, as it proved, was fortunate, as the train by some miracle was on schedule.

Entrusting Dinwiddie's brief case to the porter, I turned away as the hiss of air brakes signalized the departure of the evening southbound. My duty to Guy's guest, I felt, ended with seeing him safely aboard. And although theoretically I was on duty twenty-four hours a day, I considered myself entitled to a few minutes' relaxation and a glass of ale before my return.

I had just finished my first glass and was debating the question of a second when I heard, above the hum of traffic outside the café, the hoarse bellow of the fire whistle.

Before I could get to the sidewalk the first piece of apparatus came tearing past with a rush and a roar. I caught a glimpse of department volunteers clinging desperately to the sides with one hand and struggling to don coats or helmets with the other.

Some sixth sense, some terrifying premonition, lifted my eyes to the distant roofs of Fitch's Folly, etched clear and distinct against the pure gold of the western sky.

For a second I could not credit that the glare which met my gaze was not that of the sunset alone. It was not until, narrowing my eyes, I saw a long banner of smoke streaming skyward from the barn, that I realized that Peter Fitch's persistent prophecy had, in some portion at least, been fulfilled.

CHAPTER III
HOLOCAUST

The hook and ladder truck went screaming past as I slid in behind the wheel. I passed it a block down the street. The chemical had a better start, but I managed to squeeze by just before it turned off the ribbon of cement onto the winding dirt road leading upward through the forest to Fitch's Folly.

"They've got him!" I muttered as I fought the roaring car upward around the dizzy corkscrew loops toward the mountain top. "They've got him!"

Obsessed as I was by the fear of fire and the continual croaking of my employer anent the topic, it never occurred to me to believe otherwise. I was utterly taken aback when, as I zoomed up the long slope from the gates to the burning barn, the first person to meet my gaze was Peter Fitch, his wizened figure clearly outlined against the red glare of the roaring inferno beyond.

He turned as I skidded to a stop, well out of danger, and came skipping nimbly toward the car.

"You see, don't you, Bill?" he cried shrilly, gripping my arm with claw-like fingers of surprising strength. "Didn't I tell you? And it's just begun—just begun!"

"You mean—the fire?" I said stupidly.

"Not the fire—the fires!" shrilled old Peter. "The plot—the persecution! Thank God they didn't trap me this time!"

The heat from the blazing building was intense. I felt the muscles of my face stiffen as I forced myself to gaze into its seething depths.

"Is every one safe?" I asked in a low voice that I tried in vain to keep steady.

"Safe? Oh, yes! Safe as a church—this time! But maybe next time—"

He broke off suddenly to peer past me into the rear seat.

"Where's that son of mine?" he demanded. "Don't tell me he went off with that Dinwiddie!"

"Guy? He didn't—"

I stopped sharply, stunned. Guy had been in the barn when I left! I remembered the gleam of light I had seen. Was it—could it be—

"I saw him—in there!" I said shakily. "Are you—haven't you seen him?"

Old Peter eyed me shrewdly.

"Saw him a minute ago," he shrilled, with one of his exasperating flashes of eccentricity.

"Where?"

"Oh, somewhere around," he said with a vague gesture.

I stared about me skeptically. Most of the household, to be sure, was visible. Nellie Fitch, almost within arm's reach, was cursing heartily in a manner most unladylike. Ruth Vale, her small, pointed face as white as chalk, was just beyond, and Margery, a wild gleam in her black eyes, stood with arms akimbo on the driveway a dozen feet distant.

Karl, his arm crooked about his face, was backing blindly away from the flaming inferno. George Wold was directing a feeble dribble from a garden hose in the general direction of the fire, and even the gangling Wenty was hard at work lugging a saddle away from the barn.

But of Guy and Martha Fitch, Patty and Gilbert, I could see no sign. Nor, I recalled afterward, of Alice Lodge.

An instant later, however, Martha burst from the house and came running down the driveway, screaming. I shall always remember the hideous shrillness of her voice against the crackling background of the flames.

"Where's Guy?" she shrieked hysterically. "Where's Guy?"

She halted, her gaze sweeping the group of horrified watchers. Then, with an unearthly cry, she threw up her arms and ran directly for the burning barn.

I have often wondered if George's sudden forward movement with the garden hose had been sheer luck, or whether he had tripped her purposely. At all events, she caught her foot in it and plunged forward in a screaming heap not twenty feet from the flames.

Before she could rise he was at her side. Lifting her gently, he bore her, despite her struggles, across the driveway, beyond the spreading circle of heat, and set her gently on her feet beside me.

She struggled wildly for a moment in his grasp. Then she relaxed, her lids fluttered shut, and she slid from his arms to the grass in a dead faint.

Across her limp body George and I exchanged worried glances.

"Is Guy really in there?" I asked in a low tone.

The gardener shrugged his stooped shoulders.

"I dunno, Bill," he said gloomily, squinting sidewise at the fierce flames streaming skyward.

"But if he is—"

With bell clanging and siren screaming, the motor chemical labored into view through the gateway below and came roaring up the drive, with the hook and ladder truck in hot pursuit. The second chemical did not arrive until some ten minutes afterward, having, I later learned, unfortunately run out of gas just as it reached the foot of the hill road.

Immediately a scene of indescribable confusion ensued. The Vershire volunteers, dismounting, began running to and fro like so many ants from whose snug home a flat stone has been lifted, while Fire Chief Abel Stillwater, his lanky length up-reared from the driver's seat of the first truck, bawled unintelligible orders through his megaphone.

At length some semblance of order was attained, and approximately two thousand feet of hose were hurriedly laid from the barn to the cement reservoir farther along the ridge which furnished Fitch's Folly with water. The effectiveness of this feat was somewhat discounted when it was shortly discovered that the hose had been laid wrong end to, with the nozzle coupling at the reservoir and the strainer coupling placed ineffectually at the scene of the fire.

Meanwhile the barn blazed merrily, sending swirling showers of sparks and burning brands hundreds of feet into the air. Fortunately, it was isolated from the other buildings, which were further protected by slate roofs; otherwise the entire estate would inevitably have fallen prey. It was not until the barn roof had fallen in with a roaring crash that the harassed firemen were at length able to direct a hissing stream into the flaming embers.

I turned at a touch, to find old Peter still at my elbow.

"Damn' dummies!" he shrilled scornfully, jerking a skinny thumb toward the clustered group. "I could spit on a fire and put it out quicker'n the whole bunch of 'em! Nice sort of protection for a man living in daily dread of death!"

"How did it happen, Mr. Fitch?" I asked.

The old man shook his white-thatched head.

"No idea, Bill. I was out in the barn myself, talking to Guy, just before you went downtown. I supposed he was going down to the station with that friend of his. You're sure he didn't?"

"Of course I'm sure!" I said tartly.

Peter Fitch absently clacked his false teeth together—a hideous mannerism of which he was blissfully unconscious.

"I don't see yet how it could have happened," he said. "I was up in my room when I heard someone yell 'Fire!' I looked out and saw smoke pouring out of the windows. I grabbed up the extension phone and called the fire department—but shucks! 'Twas too late by then, even if the fire station had been next door. When I got back to the window the flames were shooting out—"

"What time was it when you called, Mr. Fitch?" demanded a voice behind us.

We both turned with a start. Police Chief Larry Frost was standing within a yard of us.

"What in hell's the idea of sneaking up like that?" old Peter fairly yelled. "Trying to scare a body to death?"

Larry grinned disarmingly, his virile features ruddily aglow in the light of the dying embers.

"Sorry, Mr. Fitch," he said. "I've been questioning some of the others, and I thought it would save you time and trouble if I listened in. What's this about your son Guy disappearing?"

The old man frowned, his wrinkled face for the moment serious.

"I heard Martha yelling something awhile ago," he said. "But if I took stock in everything Martha says—"

He broke off, chuckling slyly.

"I thought he'd gone down with Bill here," he said. "I didn't see him after Bill left, anyway."

"You just told me, you saw him after the fire started!" I burst out.

"Never said any such thing!" chirped the unpredictable old man promptly. "Hasn't he shown up yet, Chief?"

"No, Mr. Fitch," said Larry quietly. "He hasn't."

"Oh, well—maybe he's gone for a ride."

"While the barn was burning down? That doesn't sound awfully sensible, you know."

"Listen here, you—"

Fortunately, perhaps, for all concerned, the figure of Karl at this moment loomed out of the darkness.

"Guy's wife—she iss very bad, sir," he said. "It iss best that you should come at once."

Ignoring us completely, old Peter turned at once toward the house, ambling nimbly off at the heels of Karl's ramrod-like form.

Larry, lighting a cigarette, eyed me quizzically.

"What a man! What a man!" he said, shaking his head. "How you can work for a crazy coot like that is beyond me! What do you do it for, anyway?"

"Money," I said sulkily.

He stared at me for a moment, then grinned. "Where do you think Guy Fitch is?" he asked abruptly.

I shook my head, ashamed of my momentary outburst of temper.

"Search me," I answered. "It's obvious that he's not anywhere on the estate, or he'd have shown up by now. But I can't imagine why he should take a car and go anywhere at this time of night."

"We might check up on the cars, I suppose. How many are there?"

"Three. Two besides this one here."

Larry, crossing to the limousine, flashed his electric torch into the rear seat.

"Just to make sure you didn't cut Guy's throat and leave him in there," he explained, leering horribly at me. "Your boss seems pretty sure he went down with you, you know."

"Well, he didn't," I said wearily.

"Can't you take a joke, Bill? Where's the garage?"

I led the way around the corner of the house. Larry's feet crunched on the gravel of the drive as he hurried past me at sight of the building and threw the beam of his torch on the open doorway.

"Look!" he said.

My eyes widened as I obeyed. Guy's sedan was the only vehicle within. Patty's roadster—the car whose starter I had repaired that morning—was indubitably missing.

"Well, that explains it," said Larry slowly. "Or else it doesn't—I don't know which."

"Explains what?"

"Where Guy is. He and his daughter and her boy friend—"

My mouth dropped open.

"Aren't Patty and Gilbert here either?" I demanded.

"Apparently not. I've been doing a little quiet checking up—I got here right after the hook and ladder, you know. Helped carry Guy's wife into the house, and went on making myself at home. I didn't press the subject, because I didn't want to get anybody unduly worried. But just the same, it's beginning to look damned queer."

"What is?"

"Why, that the three of them should beat it just about the time the fire broke out. It makes a body think perhaps the old man's worries aren't entirely imaginary after all."

"You mean—"

I paused, thinking furiously.

"Old Peter said he was in the barn just before I left, didn't he?" I said. "Suppose Guy set it afire, thinking he had the old man trapped, and skipped when he found it didn't work?"

"Not so good, Bill."

"Why not?"

"Why wouldn't old Peter say something about it?"

"Perhaps he didn't know—and perhaps Guy thought he did!"

Larry looked skeptical.

"There's something screwy about this business, Bill," he said slowly. "But I doubt if you've hit on it there."

He stood flashing his electric torch about as if expecting it to light up some clue to the mystery. Then, snapping it off, he led the way back to the front of the house.

"Of course," he said, as I fell into step with him, "there's nothing, apparently, but Martha Fitch's hysterics to indicate that Guy might have been in the barn when it burned, and there's plenty to indicate that he wasn't. But all the same—"

Turning sharply aside, he crossed to the spot where Fire Chief Stillwater stood staring meditatively down into the smoking ruins.

"Say, Abel!" he began. "How long—"

"Why, hello, Larry!" said the lath-like fire chief affably. "Quite a fire we had, wa'nt it? Lucky we got here in time to save the house. 'Course, we had a little bad luck—"

"Listen here, Abel! How long before that will cool off enough to dig around down there?"

Stillwater eyed the embers speculatively.

"Not before morning, I guess," he answered. "That brickwork got pretty well het up. What do you want—"

"Couldn't you soak it down with water and make it sooner?"

"Ain't no more water," replied the fire chief equably. "We durned near drained old Fitch's tank as 'twas. Guess the boys would have, if I hadn't stopped 'em."

Larry hesitated.

"Any idea how the fire started?" he asked.

"Nobody seems to know. Rats, probably. Crossed wires, mebbe. Hard to tell."

Larry turned away with a grumble of disgust. I walked beside him as he moved toward his coupé, parked some distance down the drive.

"'Rats and crossed wires!'" he muttered under his breath. "A fat lot of help I'll get from Abel, if anything's really wrong!"

"Do you think something's really wrong, Larry?"

Larry, one foot on the running board, put his hand on the door of the coupé.

"God knows, Bill," he said soberly. "I've got a hunch there is—and I'm not taking any chances. I'm coming up here bright and early in the morning—and if that roadster isn't back by then, I'm going to take that cellar hole apart and make certain there's nothing down there that shouldn't be!"

My first waking recollection, after a restless and nightmarish sleep, was of Larry's parting words. Although it was little past daybreak, I rose hastily, dressed quietly, and slipped softly down the stairs and out into the dewy dawn.

Patty's roadster, I noted as I passed, had not yet returned.

Almost at once I saw, parked just within the gateway, a familiar cream-colored coupé. It was evident that Larry, on his arrival, had taken every precaution to avoid attracting attention, and my own movements unconsciously acquired added stealth. I fairly tiptoed across the grass, glancing back over my shoulder at the silent house behind me, and went hurrying down the drive toward the spot where the barn had stood.

The rank odor of charred wood assailed my nostrils as I neared, eyeing the blackened brick foundations and the splashes of molten, twisted glass in the openings which had once been basement windows.

Through one of these openings I cautiously peered downward upon the mass of slate and debris heaped high within.

Immediately my eye fell on Larry, squatting motionless in the far corner. There was something stiff and startled in his attitude that sent a chill of fear up my spine.

I tried to speak his name softly, but my voice cracked and broke. At the sound he spun about, one hand flashing back to the gun on his hip.

"It's me, Larry," I called, clearing my throat.

His gaze sought me out, and he lifted a swift finger to his lips.

"Come down here, Bill," he said, so low that I could barely catch the words. "No—around back—quiet as you can!"

Circling to the rear entrance, I picked my cautious way down the crude stone steps. Larry moved silently aside as I reached him.

"Look!" he whispered.

My blood froze in my veins as I gazed at the object before me, all but hidden by a huge segment of slate shingles which had crashed down from the roof above.

Charred though it was almost beyond recognition, it was undeniably a portion of a skeleton!

Horrified, I bent closer, peering beneath the slate.

"One of the horses?" I hazarded desperately. "It isn't—it can't be—"

Larry's headshake silenced me.

"I wish I could make myself believe that," he said. "But all the livestock was out of the barn. And besides—"

He gestured silently toward the huddle of bones. I nodded reluctantly. Though there was no clothing or other means of identification, there could be no question that the skeleton was that of a human being.

Larry's face was set and stern, his black eyes as hard and unyielding as chips of black jade.

"One question is—murder or accident?" he said. "Another—who is it?"

"Who?" I faltered.

"Guy, his girl, or her boy friend? Remember all three of them are missing!"

I stood staring dully down at the charred bones at my feet.

"What—what do you want me to do?" I muttered.

"Got an extension phone in your room?"

"Yes."

"Phone the medical referee—Doc Reefer. And tell him to get the county solicitor—he's worse than useless, but I suppose he'll want to be in on this. Get the call through as quick as you can. I don't dare to move anything until Doc gets here. And tell them to park down by the gate and slip up here on foot."

The first of Larry's questions was startlingly answered less than an hour later as the early morning sun, beaming cheerfully across the valley, struck myriads of sparkling glints from the cobwebs spread about the grass. Behind us, looming oddly against the sky above the jagged rim of brickwork about us, protruded the cupola atop Fitch's Folly, alone visible from the grim circle in the basement of the burned barn.

County Solicitor Gene Hawkins, red-faced and bewhiskered, stood bewilderedly apart, tugging at one of his sideburns, as Larry and I carefully lifted the segment of slate from the skeleton. Dr. Henry Reefer, the medical referee, bent close above the ghastly remains, cocking his huge head this way and that like a curious sparrow.

"Nothing much to see, Larry," he said without turning. "Rake the ashes after we move the bones—that may tell you something. Now let's—"

Bending, he carefully lifted the smoke-blackened skull in both hands. I was acutely aware of the emptiness of my stomach at sight of the hollow eye sockets staring blankly at the blue sky above. The fierce heat of the conflagration had destroyed every vestige of flesh, and even one side of the bony structure itself had been literally charred to powder.

A tiny tinkle caught my ear. Doc Reefer, cocking his head, shook the skull slightly. Something within rattled dully.

He turned it over, his gnarled hands shaking a little. Larry bent closer.

"My God!" he muttered. "So it's murder!"

For just above the base of the skull, clearly visible against the blackened bone, was a small round hole, no larger in diameter than my little finger!

CHAPTER IV
INQUISITION

It was five-thirty on the morning of July Fourth when we found the bullet hole in the charred skull. In the next three hectic hours Police Chief Larry Frost, confronted by his first major murder case, won my profound respect by the capable and decisive manner in which he went about the task of finding the murderer.

The Vershire police force, all told, comprised seven men besides its chief. One of these, Jim Forbes, Larry at once made acting chief by telephone. To Forbes he assigned three men, empowered him to deputize firemen and Legionaires, and placed him in sole charge of the town of Vershire with its holiday crowds and holiday traffic.

The other three regulars he summoned immediately to Fitch's Folly. Officer John Duncan he posted at the gateway with orders to admit no one. Officer Zenas Williams he placed outside the house to see that no one entered or left. As for Officer Jesse Peabody, he was at once put in charge of an additional force of firemen duly sworn in and ordered to make a thorough search of the ruins of the barn for clues or marks of identification.

Simultaneously, it seemed, Larry summoned an undertaker and despatched Doc Reefer with the skeleton and whispered instructions; gave Forbes orders to broadcast a general alarm for the three missing persons and the roadster; instructed him further to locate the mysterious Dinwiddie, either in New York or elsewhere, and have him held on suspicion; and asked that Mary Anderson and Della Dole be brought before him as soon as they arrived.

Now, at eight-thirty, he sat behind the massive, old-fashioned oak table in the library, which he had summarily preempted as temporary headquarters. Beside him sat the county solicitor, one hand plucking at his sideburns. Hawkins, a political wheelhorse whose job had been handed out as a reward by the party in power, was completely baffled, and looked it.

And beside the open window of the library, considerably to my surprise, I found none other than myself!

I never knew just what excuse Larry had given for deputizing me also, though I later learned that he had transformed my inglorious overseas record into some sort of berth in the Army intelligence service in order to give me standing with the family. Nor could I fathom, when the whole affair had run its ghastly course, of what real service I had been at any time, although Larry was insistent that I had.

Through the window, facing eastward, I could see the whole panorama of the valley, with Vershire itself, just below me, in the foreground. The clear morning air brought to my ears the renewed fusillade of fireworks as the town, still in ignorance of the tragedy at Fitch's Folly, awoke to its celebration of the Glorious Fourth.

As I sat there I realized suddenly how the shooting of the previous night had undoubtedly been accomplished without attracting attention. I recalled the aerial bombs I had heard en route to the railway station. No one, I felt certain, would have noticed an additional report.

I said as much to Larry, who had sent Karl to summon Peter Fitch. He nodded slowly, his dark eyes expressionless.

"Cinch," he said. "Easy enough to pull off another today, too, the way things are starting up down there."

I shivered slightly as the door opened to admit old Peter. He looked tired and worried, and it was obvious that the tragedy had taken its toll of his ancient nerves. But his slaty eyes were still bright and impudent as he ambled briskly into the room and took the seat which Larry indicated.

"You've heard of our find in the barn?" Larry began soberly.

Peter Fitch nodded.

"Lucky it wasn't me, eh?" he chirped.

"You were in the barn yourself last night?" pursued Larry, ignoring the pert query.

"Yes."

"Did you see your son Guy?"

"Yes. Talked with him."

"What was he doing?"

"Rubbing Dolly's hock with liniment."

"How long did you stay there?"

"Don't remember. Not long."

"Was Dinwiddie with him then?"

"No."

"Did you see anyone while you were there?"

Peter Fitch considered, clacking his dentures noisily.

"Wenty was hanging around when I went in," he admitted after a pause.

"No one else?"

"No."

"Then what did you do?"

"Came back to the house."

"And went to your room?"

"Yes."

"Were you where you could see the barn?"

"Not all the time, no."

"But you didn't see anyone enter or leave?"

The old man chuckled harshly, a tinge of malice in his extraordinary eyes.

"Saw Dinwiddie go in when Bill here took him to the train," he said.

"How long did he stay?"

"Only a few minutes."

Larry leaned back in his chair.

"According to that, then," he said, "it must have been either Wenty or Dinwiddie that killed Guy. Or you," he added significantly, provocatively.

"Killed whom?" shrilled old Peter.

"Whoever was killed. Your son Guy, for all we know yet."

The old man burst into a string of cackling curses.

"Me kill my boy?" he fairly screamed. "He'd have been a damned sight more likely to kill me!"

"Why do you say that?" rapped out Larry sharply.

"They're all against me—every last one of 'em!" squalled Peter Fitch. "Bill here can tell you that—he's heard me say so times enough! What's the idea of picking on me, for God's sake? Why don't you pick on Dinwiddie?"

Larry shot me a significant glance.

"Nobody's picking on you, Mr. Fitch," he said soothingly. "We're just trying to get things straightened out. Why do you say that about Dinwiddie? Who is he, anyhow?"

"Friend of Guy's," said old Peter with a shrug.

"You don't know him yourself?"

"Never saw him before in my life," cackled the old man surprisingly. "Up here on business, Guy said. Bad business for Guy, eh?"

"We're not even sure it is Guy," interposed Larry. "Now about this plot on your life, Mr. Fitch. Whom do you suspect?"

Old Peter's slaty eyes blazed.

"All of 'em, Chief—all of 'em!" he shrilled. "They're all trying to get rid of me—Guy, and Martha, and Nellie—yes, and even old lady Lodge! Every blasted one of 'em but that kid Patty! But I'm going to fool 'em—I'm going to make a new will one of these days! I'll show 'em a thing or two—"

He would have continued had not Larry checked him with an impatient gesture.

"That will be all for now, Mr. Fitch," he said. "Ask Karl to send Mrs. Lodge in."

But in Mrs. Lodge, escorted to the library by the straight-backed butler, Larry drew a blank. She had left the dinner table, she said, and had gone directly to her room, a chamber at the rear of the second floor. Here she had read until the tumult and shouting drew her to a front window. No, she had not gone out—she had merely stayed there and watched the fire. No, she had never seen Dinwiddie before.

"What occurred to upset you yesterday afternoon, Mrs. Lodge?" asked Larry, to whom I had confided some of the previous day's highlights that I had deemed significant.

My cheeks reddened as Mrs. Lodge eyed me fixedly before replying.

"Nothing in which you could have the slightest interest," she at length told Larry primly.

"May I be the judge of that, Mrs. Lodge?"

"You may not," replied the faded widow quietly.

Larry hesitated, rubbing his chin. Hawkins, clearing his throat, ventured to interpose.

"Er—I don't believe we need to bother Mrs. Lodge further for the present, Larry," he said diffidently.

Mrs. Lodge rose, stood eyeing Larry questioningly for a moment, and then with a formal bow departed with dignity.

The phone on the desk rang as Larry turned on Hawkins a gaze in which reproach and relief were mingled. He snatched the receiver from the hook.

"Hello?" he snapped. "Oh—Jim? What's that? No one answering Dinwiddie's description on the train between Springfield and New York? Well, then—"

He paused while the receiver crackled in his ear.

"Get after him in both places, then!" he commanded crisply. "Check up on the Dinwiddies in New York—there can't be more than a million guys with a name like that. And see if Springfield can't locate him somewhere in the city. No, I haven't been able to find out any more about him. I'll give you a ring as soon as I do."

Hanging up, he sat staring fixedly at me until I began to shift uncomfortably in my chair.

"Are you positive this Dinwiddie got on that train, Bill?" he demanded at length.

"I certainly am."

"And didn't get off again?"

I blinked as the significance of the query struck home.

"Not on my side, surely," I answered. "Of course it would have been possible for him to slip down the steps on the other side of the tracks before the train pulled out. But what would be his object in that, Larry? If he were guilty of any crime, wouldn't he want to put as much distance between himself and Vershire as possible?"

With a shrug Larry picked up the phone once more and gave the number of the police station.

"Listen, Jim!" he said. "I'd overlooked the possibility that Dinwiddie might still be in Vershire. Yes. Check on that, too, will you? And it wouldn't be a bad idea to query surrounding towns. Got his description O. K.? All right, Jim. Keep me posted."

He nodded to Karl, who had entered and was standing stiffly just inside the door.

"Mrs. Fitch," he said.

"Which Mrs. Fitch?"

"Either one, Karl," said Larry. "I meant Mrs. Peter Fitch—but the other one will do as well."

It was Peter's wife, however, who did appear, crossing the threshold with a formidable rustling of skirts. It was all too evident that she intended to carry matters with a high hand.

"Did you know Dinwiddie, Mrs. Fitch?" Larry shot at her.

"I did not," she replied uncompromisingly.

"Do you know the nature of your son's business with him?"

"I do not."

"When did you first see the fire?"

"I heard someone scream and I ran outdoors."

"Where were you at the time?"

"In my room."

"Was your husband with you?"

"I said I was in *my* room," repeated Nellie Fitch with emphasis.

"I see. And your husband was in his room?"

"Presumably."

"You could not say of your own knowledge that he was there?"

"I could not."

"Did you see your son Guy when you ran outdoors?"

"I did not."

"Do you know where he is at present?"

"I do not."

"Do you know where your granddaughter and Mr. Cooper are?"

"I do not."

"Do you know when they left?"

"I do not."

Larry, pausing, looked helplessly at Hawkins, who shook his head slightly.

"That will be all for now, Mrs. Fitch," said the police chief.

The wife of Peter Fitch, with the air of one shaking dust from her raiment, departed majestically, her protuberant eyes like glazed gray grapes beneath her heavy brows.

Larry exhaled a deep breath.

"The hell of it is," he said parenthetically, "we don't even know whose murder we're investigating—yet. I wish Doc Reefer would call up." Turning, he nodded again to Karl.

"Now Mrs. Martha Fitch," he said.

Guy's wife, hesitating on the threshold, was obviously perturbed. Her blue eyes were pouched and red-rimmed, and her whole air bespoke bewilderment and grief.

"Sit down, Mrs. Fitch," said Larry gently. "What can you tell us that will help?"

"I'm sure I don't know, Mr. Frost," said Martha brokenly.

Larry sat drumming absently on the table. "Why did you try to run into the burning barn last night?" he demanded at length.

Faint color showed itself in her cheeks.

"I don't know," she said simply. "I must have lost my head. I felt that Guy was in the barn—"

"Why did you have that feeling?"

"Because—because—"

She dabbed her sea-blue eyes with a lace handkerchief.

"I—I couldn't find him, Mr. Frost," she said brokenly. "I knew he'd gone out there, and when the fire broke out I was worried. I hunted all over the house—"

"So you think it's your husband that is murdered?" broke in Larry with calculated brutality.

Martha Fitch uttered a tiny gasp and burst unashamedly into tears.

"I'm sorry to be so upset," she sobbed. "But I c-can't help thinking—if it isn't Guy—it may be P-Patty—"

Larry stirred uneasily.

"I'm sorry, Mrs. Fitch," he said with unwonted gentleness. "Now let me ask you another thing. Did you know this man who visited your husband yesterday?"

Martha Fitch lifted her chin defiantly.

"I never saw him before," she said. "But I'm going to find out who he is. And if he is in any way responsible—"

"Your husband gave no explanation for his visit?"

"Some private business—that was all he said."

Larry's busy fingers resumed their absent drumming.

"Do you know where Guy might have gone without telling you?"

"No, Mr. Frost."

"Nor Patty and her friend?"

"I'm sorry. They didn't—"

The phone rang shrilly. Larry, with a mumbled apology, lifted the receiver.

"Hello?" he said. "Oh—hello, Doc! What's that? A male sk— Wait a minute!"

He clamped his muscular hand over the mouthpiece.

"That will be all, Mrs. Fitch," he said hastily.

Martha Fitch, eyeing the instrument curiously, made a reluctant exit. The moment the door closed Larry removed his hand from the transmitter.

"All right now, Doc," he said. "I see. Yes, I see. Pretty far gone, eh? Now the teeth—how about them? Did you check with the dentist?"

He paused, listening, and his face slowly darkened.

"All perfect?" he said incredulously. "Well, I'll be damned! And you say Guy never—"

He listening again, his features furrowed, before slowly replacing the receiver.

"Well, I'll be damned!" he repeated.

"What's wrong, Larry?" queried Hawkins. Larry's headshake was that of a man utterly discouraged.

"I had hoped," he said, "to identify the body by the teeth. But Doc Reefer just tells me that every one was perfect—not a filling in them!"

"And Guy?" I asked eagerly.

"His teeth were perfect, too. The family dentist says—"

"Well, doesn't that prove it?"

"Prove what?"

"That Guy is the victim?"

"Only indirectly."

"I don't see why you say that," objected the solicitor blankly.

"Isn't it possible, Gene," snapped Larry sarcastically, "that there is more than one man in the world without any dental work in his molars?"

"Then who is it?" asked Hawkins.

"How do I know?" shot back Larry. "It might just as well be Cooper as Fitch, the way things stand right now. If he has perfect teeth, too—"

"It might have been that tramp I saw up here yesterday morning," I suggested.

"What tramp?"

"Skinny little chap in a ragged shirt and dirty gray knickers," I explained. "He cornered my boss down by the barn, and I think he got some money. Maybe he was still here—asleep or something—"

"Red-faced bird in need of a shave?" queried Larry.

"Yes."

Larry's headshake was decisive.

"Couldn't have been him," he said. "We gave him a bunk at the station night before last."

"Why couldn't it have been him?"

Larry grinned.

"Because he had false teeth," he said. "I saw him rinsing them out under the faucet in the morning."

I pondered the problem soberly in silence.

"So what?" I demanded finally.

"So it's probably Guy, after all. But just the same—"

The sound of a motor came to my ears. I turned to the open window beside me, and my mouth fell slowly open.

The car was Patty Fitch's roadster, with Patty herself at the wheel and Gilbert beside her. And on the running board stood Officer John Duncan, whom Larry had placed on guard at the gate.

A tense silence marked their entry into the library. Officer Duncan led the way. He stood rolling on his feet, eyeing his superior doubtfully.

"You told me not to let anyone in that gate," he said uneasily. "But these two live here, and I couldn't very well stop 'em. They asked a lot of questions, but I told 'em you'd answer 'em."

"Quite right, John," said Larry with an approving nod. "Skip on back, now. I'll handle this."

The bluecoat vanished. Larry, leaning back, sat eyeing the fugitives with hard black eyes.

"Where have you two been?" he rapped out.

Patty, her brown eyes frightened, wet her carmine lips with her tongue. Gilbert put his arm protectively about her.

"What's happened here, Chief?" he asked quietly.

"Murder!" shot out Larry.

"Who?"

"We're not sure yet," said Larry, spacing his words deliberately. "But from all indications, Miss Fitch—it was your father!"

Patty stood dazed for a moment, eyeing Larry with blanching cheeks. Then, without a sound, she swayed blindly forward.

Gilbert caught her as she pitched toward the table. Holding her in his arms, he swung angrily on Larry.

"That's a hell of a way to break the news to Pats!" he said. "Especially when we'd just come back to ask his blessing—"

My mouth gaped again. Larry slid forward in his chair, his black eyes intent.

"His blessing?" he repeated slowly. "You mean—"

Gilbert nodded, his tanned face colorless.

"Yes, Chief," he said. "Pats and I—you see—we were married last night over at Campton."

CHAPTER V
CONFESSION

Patty Fitch—Patty Cooper now—lay on the brown leather couch before the huge brick fireplace, her slender body limply relaxed. She looked almost like a little girl asleep, her dark eyes closed and her pale hair, disarranged, falling about her paler face.

Beside her Ruth Vale held a bottle of aromatics. Before the table Gilbert strode jerkily to and fro, dragging furiously at a cigarette.

"Of all the hellish messes—" he muttered under his breath.

Larry sat studying the young bridegroom intently.

"Suppose you tell me all about it," he suggested.

Gilbert, pitching his cigarette into the fireplace, squared his shoulders and swung about.

"It's like this, Chief," he said, taking a deep breath. "Pats and I wanted to get married last spring. We put it up to her father and he sat on the idea—said we were too young to know our own minds and all the rest of that line. So Pats got her grandfather to invite me up here this summer—and that didn't exactly make a hit with her old man either.

"We hit him up about it again last week, and he set his foot down good and hard; in fact, he and I had some pretty hot words over it. So after that we made up our minds we'd elope. I've got a job lined up for the first of the month, and Pats was game to go ahead whatever happened.

"Bill here probably guessed why we headed for the court house yesterday morning—but if he did, he must have kept his mouth shut. We got a license—we're both of age, you see—and I dated up a minister over in Campton."

I stared blankly at Gilbert, realizing that I must have been more than ordinarily dumb to have missed the significance of that morning trip to Vershire.

"We ducked out about eight and took the roadster," Gilbert went on. "Pats had sneaked an overnight bag into it. We left right after Bill took that fellow down to the train. It wasn't quite dark, but we didn't dare to wait any longer. We headed straight for Campton and got married and put up at the hotel.

"We must have been out of sight before the fire started. We didn't know a thing about it until the cop stopped us at the gate just now. Even then it never occurred to us—"

He broke off, fumbling for a fresh cigarette.

"We figured Pats' dad would probably raise hell," he went on in a lower tone, his gaze fixed on the still figure on the couch. "But as long as Pats was game, it didn't matter a hoot to me. But now—when I think that we went away and left him just as—just at the time—"

Patty's limp figure shivered, then relaxed. Ruth held the bottle of aromatics closer.

"She's all right," Larry assured him. "Now listen here, Cooper! Are you sure you're telling everything you know about this?"

Gilbert flushed and stiffened.

"Do you mean to insinuate—"

"Guy Fitch was murdered," interrupted Larry harshly. "And you two disappeared at almost the very moment it must have happened. I'm not accusing either of you of anything. But you'll admit I'm justified in checking up on both of you, and pretty thoroughly, too!"

Gilbert, swallowing hard, was obviously choking back a desire to take his bride in his arms and tell Larry to go to hell. But his reply, when at last it came, had all the earmarks of frankness and sincerity.

"I told you about the bad blood between us," he said. "I thought it was the only fair thing to do—and besides, I knew you'd find it out anyway! But if you've any idea that we're mixed up in the murder— well, you're all wet, that's all! Do you suppose we'd have left if we'd known—"

Larry lifted a hand to check him.

"No one's being accused of anything—yet," he said significantly. "Now if you're ready to answer a few more questions—"

"Sure thing, Chief!"

"Did you know the guest Guy brought here yesterday?"

"Dinwiddie, you mean? Never saw him."

"Do you know the nature of his business?"

"No."

"Did you see Guy after Dinwiddie left?" Gilbert shook his head.

"We were both trying to duck him," he explained. "When we saw him head for the barn, we sneaked out the back way and hid behind the garage till Bill here took out the limousine. Pats was just ready to step on the starter when we saw Bill stop at the barn—"

"Then you didn't leave until after he went on?"

"No."

"You didn't stop at the barn yourselves?" Gilbert grinned wryly.

"Now I ask you, Chief," he protested. "If you were eloping with a girl, and you knew where her dad was supposed to be—would you stop and say howdy to him, or would you step on the gas?"

There was no responsive flicker of mirth on Larry's face. He sat staring at the table, drumming absently on its polished surface.

"Did you look into the barn as you passed?" he resumed.

"No."

"Did you see anyone outside?"

Gilbert's youthful face grew serious.

"I think the half-wit was there—Wenty, I mean," he said slowly. "I remember seeing him coming up from the cottage."

Larry's fingers continued their abstracted tattoo.

"Have you a gun?" he asked suddenly.

"No, Chief. Why—"

"Have you ever seen one here?"

"No. Why do you ask that? Was—"

He broke off, his face paling, at Larry's slow nod.

"Yes, Cooper. Guy Fitch was shot—shot from behind—"

A cry from the couch caused us to turn. Patty was sitting bolt upright, her brown eyes wide with horror.

"Dad . . . shot?" she gasped.

Ruth laid a hand on her arm, but Patty shook it off.

"I'm . . . all right," she said, her voice stronger. "Is that true, Chief?"

"I'm afraid so, Miss Fitch—pardon me, Mrs. Cooper."

"But how—when—"

"That's what I'm here to find out," said Larry, not ungently. "I'm hoping you can help me."

Patty rose courageously to her feet. Gilbert's arm was about her waist as she crossed slowly to the table.

"Tell me . . . what happened!" she said unsteadily. "I can . . . take it, I guess!"

Larry sketched the murder briefly. Patty took it like a thoroughbred, erect, unwavering. But the knuckles of the fingers which clutched the edge of the table showed dead white before he finished.

"Poor Dad!" she breathed, and for a moment bowed her blonde head blindly.

"Pats, darling—"

The young bride lifted her head slowly. Her voice was firm, controlled.

"Sorry, Chief!" she said. "I was in the house all the time—didn't see a thing. And Gilbert and I left before—before it happened. We must have, Chief. If I'd only known—"

She swayed slightly, her eyelids fluttering. Larry nodded quickly to Ruth.

"Before Miss Vale helps you to your room," he said, "may I trouble you a moment longer?"

"Surely."

"Did you know Dinwiddie—your father's guest?"

"No, Chief. And I'm sure I never heard Dad mention him. I've been trying to think—"

"Don't bother, Mrs. Cooper. Now tell me this: Are there any firearms on the place, to your knowledge?"

Patty's brown eyes opened wide.

"Yes," she said slowly. "Two."

"What sort of firearms?"

"Revolvers."

"Whose are they?"

"Gramp has one—an old .32 Colt. I used to see it in his bureau drawer."

"Who has the other?"

"George."

"The gardener?"

"Yes."

"Do you know the calibre?"

"No."

"Thank you very much, Mrs. Cooper," said Larry gently. "Miss Vale, will you and Mr. Cooper see that she has a chance to lie down and rest and be undisturbed? And after that, Miss Vale, will you come back here for a moment?"

But Ruth Vale, interrogated, added nothing to the information already at hand, save that she had been Patty's confidante in the matter of the elopement. Nor did Mary Anderson and Della Dole, who arrived shortly in a high state of nerves and swore jointly and severally that they had left before seven-thirty by the rear path leading to their respective homes just outside the western boundary of the Fitch estate. Nor, for that matter, did Karl.

Larry, leaning back in his chair, passed a weary hand across his forehead.

"And just where does all that get us?" he demanded of Hawkins and myself.

"Well, not very far," admitted the solicitor, worrying at a whisker.

"I'll say it doesn't! We're not even sure that the victim was Guy Fitch—and as far as the murderer goes, we're still in a fog. There's a chance, of course, that it was some outsider—Dinwiddie, for example. But in spite of all that I'm convinced myself that the crux of the crime lies right here at Fitch's Folly."

With a single decisive motion he lifted himself from his chair.

"The next thing to do," he said, "is to check on those two guns—especially George's. If his isn't a .32, it narrows the circle considerably. If it is—"

"Why do you say that, Larry?" broke in Hawkins.

Larry lowered his voice.

"Because," he said, "the bullet that killed Guy was a .32!"

Hawkins tugged perplexedly at his sideburns. "How do you know that?" he asked.

"Doc Reefer just told me. He's checking it again—it was pretty badly battered, of course—but he's practically sure of it. Well, let's go!"

On the broad screened porch outside we came upon Peter Fitch. He was reading the morning paper as unconcernedly as if he possessed not a care in the world, a pair of old-fashioned steel-rimmed spectacles perched atop his prominent nose.

"Mr. Fitch!" said Larry, pausing.

Old Peter, lowering his paper, blinked up at him inquiringly.

"Have you a revolver?"

"Yes—an old .32."

"Where do you keep it?"

"In my bureau drawer, upstairs."

"Would you mind bringing it down?"

Scowling at the interruption, old Peter trotted nimbly through the doorway and vanished up the winding staircase. Larry had begun to fidget before he finally returned.

"It's gone!" he said dramatically.

"*What?*"

"Couldn't find hide nor hair of it," chirped Peter Fitch disconsolately. "I dug into all the drawers—"

"When did you see it last?"

My employer scratched his tousled white mop in obvious perplexity.

"Dummed if I know," he said. "It's an old-timer, Chief—hasn't been used for years. I cleaned it up this spring, when things began to look bad—"

"What things?" interrupted Larry with repressed impatience.

Old Peter eyed him slyly.

"Oh, everything," he said with wily evasion. "And I had Bill buy me a couple of boxes of cartridges—"

"Of course!" I cried, smitten by sudden recollection. "It's a rimfire gun, Larry—a real relic! I remember I even had a tough time finding the right ammunition—"

Larry's face showed sudden animation.

"Let me see those cartridges!" he demanded.

From his pocket Peter Fitch produced a sealed box, extending it in one talon-like hand.

"Here's one," he said.

"Where's the other?"

"Gone."

"Are you sure?"

"No more'n I am about the gun. Ain't neither of 'em where I put 'em."

"Had the other box been opened?"

Peter Fitch hesitated, clacking his teeth.

"Yes," he said finally. "I loaded the gun with them."

Thrusting the box of cartridges into his own pocket, Larry turned to Officer Williams, who had been an open-mouthed auditor of the interchange.

"Zenas," he said with sudden decision, "I'm going to switch you off onto hunting for that gun and those bullets. It's a damned sight more important right now than what you're doing."

"O. K., Larry," rumbled the big bluecoat.

"I want you to make a thorough search of the house—every room. I'll get you some help in a little while. You understand you're looking for an old rim-fire .32 Colt and for cartridges to fit. But if you find anything else in the line of weapons or ammunition—"

"I'll bring 'em to you right smack off!" offered Williams helpfully.

"And gum up any chance of finding fingerprints! Nothing doing! You'll leave them right where they are and let me know—understand?"

Williams, abashed, turned and entered the house. Old Peter went pattering after him.

"I'll help you look, Officer," I heard his shrill cackle as the ill-assorted pair ascended the stairs. "I won't be able to sleep a wink till that gun's found. It was Guy the first time—but it may be me the next!"

Larry's elongated strides carried him rapidly over the brow of the slope leading down to the gardener's cottage. The county solicitor's dumpy legs were trotting most of the way, and even my own longer limbs had trouble in holding the pace.

Margery Wold opened the door in response to our knock. With her wild dark eyes gleaming beneath her heavy mane of coal-black hair, she looked more like a witch than ever.

"Is your husband here, Margery?" asked Larry.

"No, he ain't!" came the snappish retort.

"Has he a gun—a revolver?"

"No, he ain't!"

She made as if to slam the door in our faces. Larry expertly interposed his No. 12 shoe.

"Where is he?" he asked.

Whatever reply Margery might have made was checked by the appearance of her husband around the corner of the cottage. His cheeks seemed unusually sunken, and his bowed shoulders were more rounded than ever.

"Hello, Chief," he said, in a voice of dull hopelessness. "'D I hear you askin' 'bout my gun?"

"Yes. You have one, George?"

"Uh-huh," said the gardener gloomily. "Come in."

Margery reluctantly stood aside as he led the way across the threshold. The interior of the cottage was sloppy and untidy, with dishes in the sink, dust in the corners, and a general air of slovenliness in marked contrast with the cook's efficiency while on duty.

"Just a moment before I look at it," said Larry. "What were you two doing when the fire broke out last night?"

"Eatin' supper," said Margery sullenly. "We was most through."

"Had either of you been near the barn?"

"Not till the fire started," vouchsafed George. "Then I run up there—"

"Yes, I know. Was Wenty with you?"

"Yes," said Margery, with suspicious promptitude.

"All through supper?"

"Yes."

"Then how do you account for his having been seen near the barn just before the fire broke out?" demanded Larry sternly.

Margery would have spoken, but her husband forestalled her.

"No use tryin' to lie out of it, Marge," he said sepulchrally. "The Chief here'll find out about it anyway. Wenty was late for supper. He'd just come in when I first heard the hollerin'."

"But he don't know nothin' about the fire!" cried Margery shrilly. "He don't dast even light a match! I whaled hell out of him when he was a kid till he quit!"

Larry gave a grimace of disgust.

"Where is he now?" he asked.

"Out wanderin' around in the woods somewhere, like as not," answered Margery. "But you needn't go huntin' him up and scarin' him to death, now! He ain't got nothin' to do with it, I tell you!"

She fell into a sulky silence, eyeing us malevolently.

"Want to see that gun now, Chief?" queried George gloomily. "It's hangin' on a nail up in my room."

"What is it—a .32?"

"Yes. It's—"

We all jumped as a sharp rap rattled the door behind us. Before any of us could respond it was thrust open, and I caught a glimpse of a blue uniform.

"Say, Larry!" blurted out Officer Jesse Peabody. "What'll we do now we got through with that stuff in the cellar?"

"What did you find?"

"Nothing!"

"You're crazy!" commented Larry curtly.

"Honest, Larry! Not a sign—not even a button!"

Larry stood staring at Peabody with mounting exasperation.

"Go back and look some more," he said at length. "Get a sieve and sift the ashes. And if you don't find anything near the spot where the body was, keep spreading out in circles until you do."

Peabody, grumbling inaudibly, backed out and closed the door.

"All right, George!" said Larry, turning briskly. "Let's go!"

We followed him up the narrow stairs into the tiny bedroom. From its dormer window, glancing out, I caught a glimpse of the gleaming cupola atop Fitch's Folly.

George's gnarled finger indicated a nail driven deep into the wall beside the window. His lank face was set in lines of even deeper gloom.

"There 'tis," he said laconically.

Larry, crossing, eyed the cumbersome weapon for a moment without touching it. Then, bending closer, he sniffed inquisitively at the muzzle.

His eyes gleamed as he took a handkerchief from his pocket and lifted the revolver carefully from the nail. He broke it open, and an exclamation of triumph escaped him.

Hawkins and I crowded closer. There were six shells in the cylinder—but only five of them held bullets!

In the center of the sixth, clearly visible, was the fresh scar of the firing pin!

Larry pried the empty shell from its chamber. His black eyes fixed themselves challengingly upon the gaping gardener.

"Come clean, George!" he said sternly. "Did you fire this?"

The gardener's face was a mask of helplessness and bewilderment. His head swung slowly to and fro in dazed negation.

"Honest, I didn't, Chief!" he mumbled. "I didn't even know it had been shot off—so help me God! I hadn't any idea—"

"Who did it, then? Was it Wenty?"

We had not heard Margery noiselessly mounting the stairs in our wake. We did not know she was in the room until the sound of her voice caused us to wheel about.

She stood in the doorway, her dark eyes wild, tossing back her mane of coal-black hair from her eldritch face.

"I did it!" she said clearly.

CHAPTER VI
FOUND AND LOST

Chief Frost and Solicitor Hawkins and I, some two hours later, were seated at the table by the kitchen window, partaking of a haphazard meal served by Della and Mary in a manner far removed from Margery Wold's neat efficiency. Margery herself, placed under technical arrest following her confession, was locked in the cottage under guard by Williams, whom Larry had relieved of his duties at the big house.

Incidentally, it might be noted, the hunt for Peter Fitch's revolver had proved fruitless, and neither weapon nor ammunition could be found despite an exhaustive search of the building and premises to which members of the fire department, transferred from the barn basement, had lent their aid.

Larry, pushing back his empty plate, cast a sweeping glance about the temporarily deserted kitchen.

"Of course," he said, lowering his voice, "Margery isn't guilty. That's absurd on the face of it. She's just confessed to shield that half-witted son of hers. I wish I could get my hands on him somehow. I'd put him over the jumps in a hurry if I could!"

Hawkins blinked bewilderedly.

"You mean—she didn't do it?" he asked.

"Certainly she didn't do it! Don't be silly! But the way matters stand now, I can't very well release her—especially as long as she keeps on insisting she's guilty!"

He stopped abruptly as Della appeared, and waited until she had left by the rear entrance.

"The thing that I can't get over right now, though," he resumed, a watchful eye on the door, "is the fact that Peabody and his gang can't find a thing in the ashes!"

"They can't?" I cried incredulously.

Larry shook his head.

"Not even a trace," he said, scowling. "They're still working, but I've given up hope."

"What was Guy wearing?" asked Hawkins.

"He was wearing," said Larry slowly, "a white shirt with mother-of-pearl buttons, a pair of gray golf knickers with a monogram belt, a pair of red and gray golf hose, a pair of white golf shoes with metal eyelets, and a wrist watch with a metal link strap. In his pockets he had some change in silver and copper—his wife doesn't know how much—and a bunch of keys."

He paused significantly.

"And out of all that lot," he went on, "Peabody's gang hasn't been able to turn up even the watch and keys, to say nothing of the smaller stuff!"

"Maybe he was robbed," I hazarded. "Maybe that tramp—"

Larry's headshake stopped me.

"That might explain the absence of the watch and money—possibly even the keys," he said. "But you can't tell me that the buttons and eyelets and the belt buckle would vanish without a trace!"

I concentrated frowningly on the problem.

"You think the body was stripped, then?" I asked.

"I can't see any other explanation."

"But why?" demanded Hawkins.

Larry's fingers tapped a tattoo on the table. "God only knows," he answered soberly.

"Any suspects in view yet?" asked the solicitor after a pause.

Larry's broad shoulders lifted, then sagged discouragedly.

"For awhile I had my ideas about that pair at the Vershire Inn," he said. "Remember I mentioned them to you, Gene? They've been there for a couple of days now—just hanging around. Hard guys, or I miss my guess. But when Jim checked up on them this morning, they both had cast-iron alibis."

"What sort of alibis?"

Larry grinned across the table at him.

"Well, not the sort that you could give official approval to, Gene," he said. "They were sitting in on one of those poker games down in the basement. It started right after supper and broke up at two this morning. And neither one of them, Jim found out on the quiet, left the table for more than two minutes at a time."

He paused, drumming moodily, and his eyes grew hard.

"Someday," he said, half to himself, "some bunch from the main stem will blow in up here and pull off something real. This place is just asking for trouble, with all old Peter's money lying around loose and not even a burglar alarm to protect it. If someone ever tipped off the New York mobs, there'd be a regular marathon to see who'd get here first."

My fantastic notion anent Dinwiddie popped into my mind. I voiced it, rather diffidently.

"That's hardly sensible, Bill," said Larry drily.

"I suppose not," I admitted.

"Concede that Guy got him up here to do away with old Peter—why should he turn on Guy, shoot him, strip him, and set fire to the barn?"

Rising decisively, he jerked his head at the solicitor.

"Come on, Gene," he said. "Let's go back to the cottage and see if Wenty showed up for dinner. I told Zenas to hold him there if he did. I sure would like to locate him!"

The two departed, leaving me alone with my thoughts. But even after Mary, with a frightened glance about, had whisked away my plate and vanished precipitately, I continued to sit by the window, striving to solve some of the perplexing problems surrounding the slaying of Guy Fitch.

Mary's attitude, I might say at this point, to a certain extent typified the feeling we all experienced. The tension which before the week was out was to strain our nerves to the breaking point, was already beginning to manifest itself in furtive glances, twitching muscles, and a general tendency to be overly suspicious one of another. As for myself, the fire of the previous night had served to magnify a hundredfold the fear from which I had begun to feel I might never be free.

Chin in hand, I sat staring at the narrow band of sunlight on the floor beside me.

Who was Dinwiddie?

Why had he come to Fitch's Folly, and where was he now?

Who had fired George's revolver?

Why had Guy's body been stripped?

Where was old Peter's gun, and who had taken it?

With whom had Alice Lodge quarreled, and why?

Was it mere coincidence that Patty and Gilbert had eloped on the very night of her father's murder?

Were the pair at the Vershire Inn and the red-faced tramp I had seen at the house in some way connected with the affair?

And in the background, but overshadowing all else:

What was the nature of the mysterious menace confronting Peter Fitch?

I shook my head slowly in baffled bewilderment. Solution of some if not all of these problems seemed vital if we were to find the key to the mystery. But I had no more idea of the proper answers than if I had never entered the employ of old Peter.

Rising discouragedly, I let myself out of the kitchen and crossed the greensward in the direction of the garage. A glance in the direction of the cottage showed me Larry and his shadow, obviously empty-handed, returning slowly up the slope.

And in that very moment it occurred to me that I might very possibly be able to locate Wenty myself.

Despite the brevity of my stay at Fitch's Folly, I had learned something of the half-wit's habits—due, perhaps, to my own liking for solitary rambles in the woods. I recalled the huge pine tree on the ridge to the north of the house. More than once I had seen Wenty climbing Tarzan-like in its green branches or lying on the thick carpet of pine needles beneath, his vacant blue eyes staring blankly skyward.

With sudden decision I set out through the apple orchard toward the wooded ridge beyond. At the moment a solitary walk appealed to me strongly, and it seemed doubtful, in the present disturbed state of affairs, if my services as chauffeur were likely to be needed. Besides, I had been duly deputized by Larry, and could offer this as an excuse, should my absence be criticized.

Treading lightly, I entered the woods, following the faint path leading toward the base of the huge tree whose towering branches, stretching heavenward, dwarfed the surrounding forest.

The pungent odor of balsam was strong in my nostrils. Somewhere a squirrel scolded, and in a patch of sunlight beside the path a regal black and orange butterfly wavered erratically on lazy wings.

Through the leaves I caught sight of an eddying spiral of smoke. My soft-soled shoes made no sound as I tiptoed forward, to stop dead at the strange sight before me.

Squatting on his haunches, his back toward me, was Wenty. Directly in front of him a pillar of smoke streamed skyward.

The half-wit's body was quivering as if in the grip of some powerful emotion. Save for this, so still he crouched, he might have been some heathen idol before which a burnt offering had been placed. Irresistibly I thought of witchcraft and of black magic—and of Margery Wold.

But when, advancing noiselessly, I came to stand behind him, I literally gaped in amazement at sight of his strange occupation.

Before him was hollowed out a shallow pit, perhaps three feet in circumference and considerably less than that in depth. The excavation, in fact, extended into the moist earth beneath, and a ring of pine needles and dirt encircled it.

It was in the bottom of this pit, fed by liberal sprinklings of needles, that the blaze originated. And at sight of the foundation on which it rested I uttered an involuntary exclamation.

With a single galvanic motion Wenty leaped up, whirled, and stood gaping at me in horror, his loose mouth distended in a voiceless yell.

"What are you doing with those, Wenty?" I demanded.

For a moment he stood staring, his freckled face working strangely. Then, with a wordless cry of terror, he dashed madly away down the path in the direction of the house.

"Come back here!" I shouted with all the force of my lungs.

He must have heard, but he did not heed. Instead, putting on a fresh burst of speed, he vanished like a scared rabbit into the underbrush.

Though strongly tempted, I did not follow. Instead, I devoted my energies to stamping out the flames at my feet, cringing as the choking smoke billowed up about me. It was not until the last spark had been extinguished that I was able to see clearly that which lay at the bottom of the shallow pit.

Dirt-smudged and sprinkled with needles, yet little damaged by Wenty's bonfire, lay a white shirt, a pair of gray knickers, and a pair of red and gray golf socks. And beside them, at one end of the excavation, stood two golf shoes!

The shock of this discovery was driven from my mind by a startled shout from the direction of the house, followed by a thrashing in the bushes and the sound of angry voices. They ceased abruptly, leaving me torn between a desire to seek their source and a wish to remain on guard over my precious find.

But before I could decide the bushes parted and Larry appeared, holding Wenty's right wrist in an iron grip.

"What's up, Bill?" he called out. "What's Wenty trying to run away for?"

"Come here and you'll see," I said soberly.

At sight of the buried clothing he emitted a long, low whistle. His face hardened as I told him what I had seen, and Wenty began to blubber beneath the merciless black eyes of his captor.

"What did you bury these for, Wenty?" he demanded sternly.

"Didn't bury 'em," muttered the half-wit.

"What's that?"

"I didn't bury 'em!" squalled Wenty. "I dug 'em up!"

"Dug them up?" repeated Larry incredulously.

"Uh-huh."

"How did you know they were here?"

"I ain't a-goin' to tell," said Wenty sullenly.

"What did you do with the watch and the money?"

Wenty clapped a startled hand to the side pocket of his ragged coat. Then, with a wary glance, he thrust both hands into his trousers.

"I dunno nothin' about 'em," he mumbled.

Larry expertly corralled his other wrist.

"Search him, Bill!" he ordered.

In a moment Guy Fitch's wrist watch was in my hand, together with a miscellaneous collection of change totaling, I believe, ninety-four cents.

Wenty, his lower lip protruding, eyed me malevolently as I pocketed them.

"Findin's keepin'," he mumbled. "You ain't got no right to take that."

"Why were you trying to burn those clothes?" pursued Larry.

"They wa'nt no good to me."

"Why not?"

"Somebody'd know whose they were," explained Wenty ingenuously.

Larry rolled toward me a baffled and despairing eye. I, for one, did not envy him his task. It was obviously impossible to sift fact from fancy as it rolled from the tongue of the gangling creature who stood before us, round blue eyes vacant, lower lip pendulous, freckled features twitching beneath its mop of carrot-hued hair. By some obscure and incongruous mental process I was reminded of my employer in one of his more difficult moments.

"Now listen here, Wenty," said Larry slowly and distinctly. "Do you know what happened to Guy Fitch?"

"Uh-huh," said Wenty surprisingly.

"What?"

"He was shot."

"Do you know who shot him?"

"I ain't a-goin' to tell," grinned Wenty engagingly.

"Did you see someone in the barn with him last night?"

"Uh-huh."

"Who was it?"

"I ain't a-goin' to tell."

Angered beyond measure at the senseless repetition, Larry seized Wenty by the shoulders and shook him until he began to blubber again.

"Do you know anything about Peter Fitch's gun?" he demanded.

"Huh?"

"Did you take it?"

"Take what?"

"A gun—a revolver—out of old man Fitch's bureau," said Larry between set teeth. "It's gone. Where is it?"

Wenty gaped at him blankly. Larry drew a deep breath of despair.

"You know your father's gun?" he began again.

"Uh-huh."

"Did you ever fire it off?"

A look of low cunning distorted Wenty's gargoyle features. He shook his carrot-thatched head violently.

"Maw said she'd whale hell out of me if I ever touched it," he said.

"But you fired it off just the same?"

Wenty's mouth flew open in amazement. "How'd you know?"

"Oh, I know, all right," said Larry, repressing elation at the success of his random shot. "But I won't say anything to your mother if you'll tell me all about it."

Wenty's vacuous face brightened with pleasurable reminiscence.

"It was last night," he said with animation. "And all them fellers down to the village was shootin' 'em off—Bang! Like that! So I sneaked in and got Paw's gun down off the nail. And I shot it off, too—Bang! Like that!"

"Did you shoot it more than once?"

"Naw. It hurt my hand, and I was afraid Maw'd find out. So I put it back—"

"Where did you shoot it?"

Wenty eyed his inquisitor shrewdly.

"'Twa'n't in the barn," he said. "'Twas outdoors."

Larry, rolling hopeless eyes heavenward, tightened his grip on the half-wit's shoulders.

"Now listen, Wenty," he said sternly, "and I'll tell you just what you did. You took your father's gun, and you went up to the barn where Guy Fitch was. You pointed it at him, and it went off—Bang! Like that! And then you set fire to the hay—"

"Didn't neither!" flared Wenty. "Maw won't let me light matches! She told me she'd—"

"She won't let you shoot guns, either," Larry reminded him.

Wenty fell silent, sucking sulkily at his nether lip.

"You shot Guy Fitch," resumed Larry, "and you might as well own up. If you don't, we'll have to lock you up—"

"*No! No!*"

Wenty strained backward, all but upsetting his captor.

"I ain't a-goin' to be locked up!" he protested. "Old Fitch told me so himself! Long's I don't do anything wrong—"

"But you were up at the barn, weren't you?"

"Uh-huh."

"And you saw someone?"

"Uh-huh."

"Who was it?"

"I ain't a-goin to tell!" repeated Wenty triumphantly.

Larry's eyelid flickered as he turned toward me.

"If he won't tell us," he said, his voice heavy with regret, "I'm afraid we'll have to lock him up anyway. If he'd only tell us, maybe he wouldn't have to go to jail."

Wenty's loose-muscled face screwed itself into a knot of painful concentration.

"If I tell you somebody, I won't have to be locked up?" he asked artfully.

"No, Wenty."

"Honest Injun?"

"Honest Injun," repeated Larry gravely.

Wenty leaned forward, his freckled face a mask of guileful cunning.

"It was Peter Fitch!" he whispered.

"Peter Fitch?"

"Uh-huh now will you let me go?" said Wenty all in one breath.

"How do you know it was?" asked Larry, looking discouraged.

"I saw him in the barn," elaborated Wenty painfully. "He shot him—Bang! Like that! And then and then he took his clothes off of him and brought 'em out here an'—an' buried 'em! An'—say—won't you let me go now?"

"Not just yet, Wenty," said Larry wearily. "I want to have a talk with your folks first."

"You ain't goin' to tell Maw about me shootin' off Paw's gun?" queried Wenty anxiously. "She said she'd whale   "

"I'll see that she doesn't hurt you," promised Larry. "Come on, now—let's go!"

Margery must have been watching from the window. She met us at the door, pushing Williams aside as if he had been a wax clothing dummy—which, in more ways than one, he resembled.

"What have you been doing to my boy?" she demanded, her black eyes blazing. To her the halfwit, though nearly thirty, seemed still a mere child—which mentally, of course, he was.

"It's all right, Maw," Wenty hastened to reassure her. "He ain't goin' to tell you nothin' about me shootin' off Paw's gun last night. He promised—"

The color slowly drained from Margery's face. "What did you say, son?" she said in a sickly tone.

Wenty, clapping his hand over his mouth, tittered foolishly between his fingers.

"Aw, gee, Maw!" he remonstrated. "I wasn't goin' to—"

"Run into the cottage a minute, Wenty," ordered Larry, jerking his thumb at Williams. "I want to talk to your mother."

He turned to Margery as the door closed behind the pair. The cook's belligerence had utterly evaporated. She seemed suddenly stricken, and her black hair framed a face filled with dull hopelessness.

"Margery," he said, not unkindly, "your boy's mixed up in this affair somehow—I don't know how. I don't want to lock him up, but I can't have him running around here loose till we get things straightened out. Now I'll tell you what I'm going to do—what I've got to do. I'm going to get a couple of doctors up here right away and have Wenty sent to the State hospital for observation. It's only about thirty miles to the capital, and you and George can see him whenever you want to."

Margery stood staring at him with lifeless eyes.

"I fired that gun," she said, but there was no conviction in her tone.

Larry shook his head pityingly.

"I'm sorry, Margery," he said, "but it's no use. Don't worry, now. They'll treat Wenty fine down there. Maybe they'll be able to help him."

Without a word she turned and entered the cottage, from which Williams at once emerged.

"Stay here and keep an eye on them, Zenas," ordered Larry. "I'll be back in a few minutes."

Stopping only long enough to phone Doc Reefer regarding Wenty, he hurried back down the path toward the big pine. I was close at his heels as he burst into the open space beneath the overhanging boughs.

The next instant I nearly tripped over his legs as he halted suddenly, staring.

"My God!" he breathed. "They're gone!"

The shallow pit in the pine needles was empty. Guy Fitch's apparel, which we had both seen there within the half hour, had disappeared!

CHAPTER VII
ROBBERY

Larry smacked a furious fist into the palm of his hand.

"Of all the prize boobs!" he grated. "And to think that I didn't have brains enough to either leave you here or have you bring them along!"

The next quarter hour or more was devoted to a frantic search in the vicinity of the big pine and a furious burrowing beneath the thick carpet of needles. But the clothing Guy Fitch had worn the previous day had vanished without a trace.

At length, giving over the fruitless quest, Larry straightened and stood staring blackly at me. His hands were covered with dirt and his forehead was wet with sweat and wrinkled with worry.

"Well, that's that!" he said bitterly. "Better look in your pockets, Bill, and see if you've still got the watch and change! Like as not you'll find they've been lifted while you and I were mooning around like a pair of nitwits!"

The coins and timepiece, however, were still intact. Larry, taking possession of them, thrust them deep in his trousers pocket.

"Now let's get out of here ourselves," he said glumly, "before somebody comes along and kidnaps us!"

As we neared the house old Peter came hurrying to meet us, his slaty eyes crackling with anger.

"What's this about Wenty being taken away?" he shrilled. "Doc Reefer and Doc Slade just came! Said they were going to examine him—said 'twas your orders—"

"Where are they now?"

"Down at the cottage. What's the idea— Hey, hold on!"

Larry, ignoring him, had broken into a run. Old Peter, furious, stood glaring after him as he disappeared over the brow of the hill.

"Get the car out, Bill!" he shrilled, wheeling back. "I'm going to see Judge Manning and have a stop put to this right away—understand? Wenty's a good boy—he never hurt a fly! Well, come on—what are you standing there for?"

By virtue of my trip to town I was compelled to miss Wenty's departure. From this trip, I judged by old Peter's furious mutterings on the return ride, he had derived scant satisfaction. And yet, incongruously enough, his anger seemed oddly mixed with an air of suppressed exultation, and now and then a little chuckle escaped his leathery lips.

At the time I blamed my own impatience for the feeling that his visit to the judge's office had been inordinately protracted. It was not until later that I was to realize that my impatience had had justification in fact.

Larry, dropping in for a cigarette just before supper, apprised me of some of the afternoon's missing links.

"The queerest thing," he said, inhaling deeply, "was the way Wenty acted. I had another talk with him before they took him away—that is, I tried to. But he acted as if he were having some sort of a spell."

"What do you mean?"

"He'd shut up like a clam," Larry explained. "Wouldn't say a word. Denied he ever saw anybody in the barn or knew anything about the clothes under the tree. I'm going to drive over and see him in the morning, unless something turns up in the meantime. Maybe he'll be ready to talk again by then—even if he doesn't talk sense."

"How'd you come out with my boss?" I inquired. "He was fit to be tied the last time I saw him."

"Oh, he put up a squawk, but it didn't get him anywhere," said Larry, thus negligently disposing of one of Albany's richest residents. "I guess the judge must have told him we were within our rights. Anyway, he hasn't sworn out a warrant against me yet."

He squashed out his cigarette and sat drumming absently on the arm of his chair.

"Why should Wenty say he saw him in the barn?" I ventured.

"Search me," said Larry, shrugging. "Why should a crazy man say all the crazy things he does?"

Rising, he walked to the window and stood staring at the far blue ranges, above which the westering sun seemed to hover by a bare hand's breadth.

"Sometimes I wonder," he said, half aloud, "just what he did see in the barn last night. Sometimes I wonder if he didn't really see Peter Fitch."

I laughed a little nervously at the notion.

"You're kidding," I said.

"I suppose I am, Bill," he said slowly, turning. "Maybe it's nerves. I don't like the way things look up here at all. I'm staying myself to-night—not that I really expect anything more to break, but it's best to play safe. And by morning some of the lines we've got out ought to give us something real to work on."

I carried Larry's fantastic notion that night into my dreams, which limned old Peter as a fiend incarnate, burning and slaying indiscriminately and with a cold fury which left me terrified and powerless. He was advancing with a huge, blazing torch to fire the garage when a furious knocking sounded upon my locked door.

I leaped from my bed, gasping and sweating and not more than half awake.

"Who is it?" I demanded between chattering teeth.

"It's Larry! Open up! There's been hell to pay!"

I snapped the bolt back and threw open the door.

"What is it?" I cried as he entered.

Larry's unshaven jaws were clamped tightly together, and his black eyes glinted darkly.

"It's old Peter!" he grated.

"Dead?" I demanded, aghast.

"No, he's not dead, Bill—but he's next door to it. I found him bound and gagged on the floor in front of his safe in the library. The safe door was open and everything cleaned out—about twenty thousand, his wife thought."

"Did he tell you what happened?"

Larry shook his head soberly.

"It's a question if he'll ever be able to," he said. "Doc Reefer's been working on him for half an hour, but he's still unconscious."

But Peter Fitch, this time at least, was to fool both death and Doc Reefer. By mid-forenoon, spurning the suggestion of bed, he was sitting indomitably erect in the straight-backed chair in the corner, narrating his hideous experience of the previous night.

I could not help marveling anew at the old man's astounding vitality. His skinny wrists beneath their bandages had been worn raw by his fruitless struggles against bonds fashioned from the telephone cord, which even now a repair man from the Vershire office was replacing; and his leathery cheek still showed a red weal where one end of the court plaster gag had been too roughly removed. But his tousled white head was still unbowed, and his slate-colored eyes, set in their skein of fine wrinkles, glittered with all their old fire.

Despite the vicious attack to which he had been subjected, there was seemingly about him an air akin almost to relief. Was it, I wondered, because the hidden danger on which he had so incessantly harped had at last assumed tangible form? Did he welcome the chance to meet it in the open after weeks, perhaps months, of secret and gnawing fear?

His story, when it had been told, afforded meager clues. Lying sleepless, sometime past midnight, he had thought he heard a noise on the lower floor. He had accordingly risen, donned bathrobe and slippers, and gone softly down the stairs.

The library door, he said, had stood ajar, and he had entered. In the dim light from the windows he had caught a fleeting glimpse of a shadowy figure kneeling before the safe. Then, without warning, had come crushing blackness and oblivion.

He had revived to find dawn at hand, the room empty, the safe door open, and himself lying on the floor, hands and feet tightly bound with telephone cord, mouth sealed with surgeon's plaster. His circulation had been cut off, and his limbs were numb and nearly paralyzed. For a time he had fought fiercely to free himself, only to sink at last into the coma in which Larry, an hour later, had found him.

But the startling fact, which to me at least definitely linked the attack on Peter Fitch with the burning of the barn, was the discovery in one corner of the library of a wire waste-basket filled to the brim with charred papers, in which his assailants had evidently kindled a fire. The floor beneath was scorched, and it seemed little less than a miracle that the blaze had burned itself out without doing further damage.

Of this, however, old Peter knew nothing. He had noted, he said, no light or fire of any kind.

"Was the person at the safe anyone you'd ever seen before?" Larry asked.

Old Peter clattered his dentures belligerently.

"I got no idee, Chief," he said. "They had their back to me—"

"Was it a man, or a woman?"

"Might have been either one, for all I know. I didn't get more'n a peek at them."

"And you didn't see the one that sandbagged you?"

"Never suspected there was another one!" the old man shrilled. "It all happened so quick—"

"How much money was there in the safe?"

"About twenty-five thousand dollars," said old Peter, looking decidedly sick at the thought.

"Why do you keep so much money in the house? Don't you realize how dangerous it is?"

"I got more'n twice as much as that left here yet," cackled old Peter triumphantly.

"Where is it?"

"Where nobody'll ever find it!" was the quick retort.

Larry lowered his gaze to the table before him, on which his fingers were drumming absently.

"Whom do you suspect, Mr. Fitch?" he asked without looking up. "Or haven't you any suspicions?"

The old man's disturbing eyes narrowed craftily.

"I'm not saying who I suspect!" he burst out. "But just as sure as I'm sitting here, somebody in this house had a hand in it!"

"You mean—one of the servants?"

Old Peter, blinking, sat stubbornly silent. He might have been a graven image save for the flicker of his wrinkled lids.

"Surely you don't believe some member of your own family involved?" persisted Larry.

"I'm not saying what I think!" piped Peter Fitch, in a manner oddly reminiscent of Wenty's defiance of the previous afternoon. "It's your job to find out who's involved! But if I was in your place, I'd start my hunt right here at Fitch's Folly!"

"It's a tough one, all right," said Larry half to himself after my employer, limping but untamed, had left the library. "I've already got everyone in the house fingerprinted. There's not a mark on the safe but his, nor one in the room that doesn't belong to someone here. Even the knife used to cut the phone cord hasn't a mark on it. And the court plaster—"

"Where did that come from, Larry?" interrupted Hawkins, who had been sitting dumbly in the corner.

Larry shook his head wearily.

"I don't know," he said. "They tell me there was a roll—or part of one—in the medicine chest. Now it's gone. Miss Vale says she used it up day before yesterday when Miss Fitch—Mrs. Cooper, I mean—chafed her heel with some new golf shoes."

"What does Mrs. Cooper say?" asked Hawkins.

"Oh, she tells the same story—says she took it off yesterday afternoon and threw it away. That means—unless they're lying together—that the plaster was brought in by someone outside. I've had the house searched again, but it didn't show up—nor the revolver, nor Guy Fitch's suit, for that matter."

He passed his hand over his forehead, brushing back his crisp black locks, and looked across the table at me.

"I can't help feeling there's something screwy about all this, Bill," he said. "If he's so sure it's somebody here in the house—why doesn't he come out and tell us whom he suspects? I used to have the idea he had a persecution complex of some sort—but last night certainly doesn't look like it!"

"But who up here would attack an old man like that?" objected Hawkins, once more worrying his whisker.

"Who wouldn't, you mean!" corrected Larry. "As near as I can make out, there's little love lost between Peter Fitch and any of the rest of the family—"

"Except Patty," I reminded him.

Larry looked thoughtful.

"That's true, of course," he said. "If this were a detective story, I suppose she'd be the proper one to suspect, being the least logical. But I can't exactly figure what she would gain by it—or she and Gilbert, for that matter. From all accounts her grandfather would give her the earth with a fence around it, if she only went and asked him for it."

He pulled the repaired telephone toward him.

"Can you find out for me," he asked the chief operator, "exactly what time in the morning this line went bad? Was a note made of it? Two-fifteen, you say? Thanks."

He replaced the receiver, his restless fingers absently active.

"Well, that doesn't prove anything, either," he muttered. "The old man didn't know what time he came downstairs. I wonder— *Say!*"

Snatching up the phone once more, he barked the number of the Vershire police headquarters.

"Listen, Jim!" he snapped. "Check on those two birds at the Inn— you know the ones I mean! See if they're still there, and what they were doing last night, and if they can prove it! And ring me back right away! Oke!"

At the end of fifteen minutes Acting Chief Jim Forbes called. His reply was highly informative.

The two men, whose names appeared on the hotel register as A. B. Brown and S. Robinson, both of New York City, had not been seen the previous night after they had gone to their room. The night clerk, however, admitted occasional naps, and could not give them an absolute alibi.

Shortly before six o'clock that morning the two had appeared in the lobby with their luggage, had checked out without waiting for the dining room to open, and had been seen heading southward at high speed.

CHAPTER VIII
CONFIDENCES

Within another fifteen minutes the names of A. B. Brown and S. Robinson, together with their descriptions and the license number of their sedan, were on their way out over the wires to police headquarters in towns and cities throughout New England.

"Not," said Larry bitterly, "that it's likely to do any good."

"Why not?" asked Hawkins inanely.

"Well, in the first place, Gene—it's only a guess that they're mixed up in it at all. And in the second place—if they are, it's a cinch they're all fixed up with fake numbers and a hideout to head for. But we'll go through the motions, anyhow."

Acting Chief Forbes, incidentally, had also reported that the New York police department had declared definitely that no such person as Dinwiddie, to their knowledge, existed.

"We're only small fry up here—just a bunch of hicks," commented Larry scathingly. "They don't give a damn for us. They run our query through the mill, and some fathead grabs it and looks at it and says 'Wire 'em "No."' And some other fathead does it, and—oh, well, it's all a big help!"

He pulled himself doggedly to his feet. The hands of the grandfather's clock in the corner, I noted, stood at ten-thirty.

"I've got time to take a run down to the State hospital before dinner," he said. "I told Wenty's folks I'd fix it so they could see him tonight. Maybe he'll be ready to loosen up and talk by now. I'll swear he's guilty of something, if it's nothing more than suppressing evidence—not that the poor nut's evidence would be worth a damn in court!"

He flung out of the house, and a moment later his cream-colored coupé went careening down the mountain side in a cloud of dust.

I stood on the porch staring after it, feeling the hot July beating down upon my weary head—which, after all, felt sufficiently addled without this added aid.

Dinwiddie, Brown and Robinson, Alice Lodge, Patty and Gilbert, Martha, Nellie, Wenty, Karl, George and Margery—what part, if any, did all these play in the reasonless riddle of Fitch's Folly?

I was able to add another kink to the tangled skein a moment later. Crossing to the garage, I caught sight of Peter Fitch conversing with a man at the rear of the house whom I recognized as the skinny, red-faced tramp I had seen the previous week.

As I looked, something passed between them. I felt certain it was money, for the tramp, grinning and ducking his head, backed away and disappeared around the corner of the house.

Puzzling over this fresh problem, I mounted the stairs to my room, blistering hot beneath the summer sun, and busied myself with the shave for which I had not had time that morning. I was rinsing my razor when a knock sounded on the door behind me.

"Come in!" I yelled.

The door opened, but no other sound followed. I spun about, and all but dropped the razor to the floor.

On the threshold stood Ruth Vale, her dark eyes fixed upon me with an odd expression which I could not interpret. Even her voice, when she spoke, sounded a trifle strained.

"Will you have time to drive me down to the post office before luncheon, Bill?" she asked. "I have some letters here which should go on the noon train."

A moment before, so deep had my interest in the mystery become, I would have felt sharp resentment at any errand which might remove me, even temporarily, from the scene of the crime. But this was something decidedly different.

"Certainly, Miss Vale," I said. "Or, if you prefer, I'll take them down and mail them for you."

Her expression did not change, but her voice revealed definite embarrassment.

"I'd rather take them myself, I think," she said.

Inwardly cursing myself for an awkward fool, I put away my razor, which I found at the moment still firmly gripped in my right hand. Donning my coat and cap, I followed her down the stairs and opened the rear door of the limousine.

To my surprise, she shook her head quickly.

"If you don't mind," she said, lowering her voice, "I'll ride in the front seat with you."

Deeply puzzled but nothing loath, I nodded assent. I could not help wondering, as we drove past the house, what comment the unconventional seating arrangement might cause.

From the corner of my eye I stole an occasional glance at my passenger as I let the limousine roll easily down the winding road toward the forest below. Her blue-black hair, brushed straight back from her white forehead, accentuated the alluring lines of the attractive, almost pointed little face below. A vague, elusive scent pervaded the car. I could think of nothing but new-mown hay, unless it was the baskets made of sweet grass which my aunt had kept in the parlor.

The pleasure her presence beside me inspired brought forcibly to my mind my present menial status. For almost the first time since release from my unjust imprisonment, a spark of ambition kindled within me.

Perhaps it was not too late, even now, to rehabilitate myself. Perhaps, if I were not a chauffeur—

A touch on my arm demolished my daydream. I turned, to find Ruth's bright dark eyes fixed almost imploringly upon me.

"Would—would you mind stopping a minute, Bill?" she asked unsteadily. "I've just got to talk to somebody!"

We were not more than a hundred yards below the gates, but a curve in the road screened us from view by Officer Duncan, again on guard at the entrance to the grounds. In blank bewilderment I pulled out at the side of the narrow road, shut off the engine, and turned toward her.

"Very glad to be of any assistance, Miss," I assured her, my tone hopelessly wooden with awkwardness and embarrassment.

She sat silent for a moment, plaiting her slim fingers nervously together in her lap. Then, lifting her eyes, she smiled shakily—a brave, piteous smile that left me breathless.

"Bill," she began, "you haven't always been a chauffeur—have you?"

"No," I replied blankly.

"What did you do before that?"

"Oh, different things."

"Did you ever have any experience with—oh, courts, and crime, and that sort of thing?"

I hesitated, baffled and a little suspicious. As it happened, I had had both kinds since leaving the Army—six years as a Federal investigator with a bureau which I need not name, and six months in a Federal prison after the man I had believed my best friend had framed me for his own crime. But I failed to see why these facts should interest her, or what bearing they had on the case in hand.

"A little," I said cautiously. "Why?"

"Oh, I don't know. You look so capable and dependable and—nice, somehow. And I just must have some advice, and I don't know whom else to ask. The Chief is so hard and efficient he frightens me sometimes. And that other man—Hawkins—he's just plain dumb!"

She wrinkled her adorable nose in disgust, and I could not restrain an appreciative grin. But the next instant she was once more deadly serious, and her first words sent a chill of apprehension through me.

"Supposing," she said slowly, "that I knew something about this case—something which might have something to do with the murder of Patty's father. Should I volunteer it without being asked?"

"What do you mean?" I inquired, sparring for time.

"Supposing," she explained, "that it involved some member of the family—that if it came out, it was likely to get them into trouble—"

She broke off, her slim fingers twisting nervously.

"Oh, I can't believe it had anything to do with it!" she cried with sudden vehemence. "It's not possible! I'd feel like a traitor if I told! And still I can't get it off my mind! I keep thinking—"

"Something you saw or heard?" I suggested.

"Both," she nodded. "Something I wasn't supposed to see or hear."

"Suppose you tell me in confidence, Ruth," I began, and broke off in confusion. She had been "Ruth" so often in my thoughts that it had slipped out inadvertently.

She appeared not to have noticed. She sat with bitten lips, her dark eyes lowered. Then, with sudden decision, she lifted them to my face.

"It was Guy—and Gilbert!" she burst out, and stopped short.

"Gilbert?" I repeated.

"It was just before he went out to the barn—Guy, I mean," she continued, the words coming with a rush. "He caught Patty coming out of her room—I'd been helping her pack. I was still in the room, but he didn't see me. She told him what she was going to do, and he called her—well, never mind what.

"And just then Gilbert came up. He'd heard what Guy said. He grabbed Guy by the shoulder, and Guy swung around and struck him in the stomach and knocked him down.

"I could see Gilbert's face through the crack in the door when he got up. It was white and queer looking, and his eyes were—oh, terrible!

"'You'll be sorry for that!' he said. 'I'll find a way to make you sorry—some time when Pats isn't around!'

"I slipped out of the door and went back to my room. I was shaking all over, just remembering Gilbert's face.

"I looked back when I got to my door. Guy had turned away, and Patty was hanging onto Gilbert's arm.

"Apparently she forgot all about what I'd heard. She never mentioned it to me afterward—even after they came back and found him dead. But I haven't been able to forget it. Gilbert's temper is sometimes terrible—I saw him in a rage once at school last spring, just after he and Patty had had a hideous row."

Her dark eyes widened, and her voice fell lower.

"Ever since," she said haltingly, "I can't help thinking—if he'd followed Guy out to the barn—and slipped in somehow without being seen—"

She broke off suddenly, and her dark eyes brimmed with tears.

Involuntarily my arm went about her shoulders. Strangely, she did not resent it. Rather, she seemed to nestle closer in an unconscious gesture of trust and confidence.

"What shall I do, Bill?" she sobbed. "Oh, it's driving me crazy! I can't let Patty down that way! And yet—"

I tightened my arm reassuringly.

"Ruth," I said, using her name deliberately, "if I were in your place, I'd do nothing about it for the present. You're not concealing any actual knowledge of the crime—only a possible motive. And as I see it, until we've checked up on a lot of other things, to tell might do you more harm than good."

Before the affair at Fitch's Folly had ended, I was to remember her broken answer.

"You don't know—how true—that is!" she sobbed.

At the time, however, I attributed it to mere hysteria. I patted her slim shoulder comfortingly, and gradually her sobs died to a mere sniffle.

"You're a dear, Bill," she said, looking up at me with a gaze which I found difficult to resist. "You've no idea how much it's helped to talk it out with you like this. Now let's drive on, before someone catches us sitting here like a couple of parkers."

By tacit consent the topic was dropped during the remainder of our trip, being replaced by an informal and inconsequential conversation which at the time I enjoyed hugely. But later, as I ate with the silent Karl in the kitchen, sober reconsideration left me in something of a quandary.

I was less puzzled, I admit, as to whether I had advised her aright than as to why she had sought my advice. My scarred cheek had made me something of a recluse as far as girls were concerned, and I could imagine no valid reason why she should single me out for her confidences. As for the obvious thought that my show of interest in her might have aroused a reciprocal feeling on her part, it never entered my head.

Unwillingly, then, I admitted the possibility of double-dealing. What if she had confessed this much under seal of secrecy in order to shield Patty and Gilbert from even more direct implication in Guy Fitch's murder? What if she herself were somehow involved in the ghastly business, and sought to create camouflage by casting suspicion on Gilbert?

What if—I thought of this with a start—what if Guy had been already dead when Dinwiddie visited the barn? Had that caused Dinwiddie's hasty exit, his silence on the trip down the mountain, his disappearance?

I had reached no conclusion when Larry arrived, hot and irritated, shaving made the sixty-mile trip and a call at the State hospital in well under two hours.

"And still he won't talk!" he grated, slamming the door behind him and dropping into a chair. "Somebody's been telling him to keep his mouth shut—and ten to one it's Margery! If I thought she was really involved—"

His careworn countenance cheered appreciably as Della set a heaping plate before him, and he attacked its contents with gusto.

"I've arranged for his folks to see him tonight," he said indistinctly as I rose. "They're to be there at eight. I've arranged with Dr. Schmalz for a dictaphone record of their talk with Wenty. I don't expect much from it, but anything's worth trying."

"Am I supposed to drive them over?" I asked glumly.

"No. I've fixed it with the Vershire Taxi. I want you right here tonight. I'm going to be here, too—and not up in the corner room on the second floor, either. If I hadn't slept so damned sound, I might have horned in on last night's ruckus."

"Then you're expecting more trouble tonight?" I asked, lowering my voice.

Larry shrugged his broad shoulders.

"We've had it two nights running," he retorted. "Might as well figure on the third, hadn't we?"

The afternoon, however, was one of outward serenity. Save for a trip to the library with Mrs. Lodge I found myself unoccupied, with plenty of time to ponder the increasingly complicated problem propounded by Guy Fitch's death. But all my ponderings proved fruitless, and a fresh development served only to accentuate my headache.

Martha Fitch, attired in hastily purchased mourning, had accompanied Alice Lodge to the library. Straining my ears unashamedly, I was dumbfounded to hear her tell her aunt en route that she had discovered, in some manner which she would not state, the true identity of her husband's pre-holiday visitor!

"But don't you breathe a word of it, Aunt Alice!" she warned. "I can't imagine what he was here for—but I'm going to find out! And when I do—"

I have never known how she obtained her partial knowledge—a letter, possibly, though we found none. I have never understood why, after swearing her aunt to secrecy, she saw fit to broadcast the fact that night at dinner, as I heard her through the open window. To show, probably, she had information not generally known, and to strike terror to the heart of the person whom she even then may have vaguely suspected of Guy's murder.

Under the storm of questions that beat about her at the dining table she sat silent, her lips compressed, shaking her faded blonde head determinedly.

"I'm not saying anything now—even to the police," she said. "I mean to find out more about it first. And when I do—"

I have often wondered what would have happened had I gone to Larry, as doubtless I should have done, with the fruits of my eaves-dropping. Would she have told him what she knew, or would she have refused? And if she had refused, would he have been far-seeing enough to act?

We shall never know.

Larry himself was not idle as the afternoon wore on toward the glorious sunset which marked the advent of our third night of terror. His chief activity was to despatch a trusted messenger to New York, bearing with him the bullet taken from Guy Fitch's skull, to consult a noted ballistics expert. The bullet, it seemed, continued to be a baf-fling and inexplicable factor, and Doc Reefer was now unwilling to say whether or not it had been fired from George Wold's revolver.

At seven-thirty, with the western sky behind us a gorgeous mass of flame-colored cloud, he called us together at the garage and out-lined his plans for the night. George and Margery, incidentally, had left more than a half hour earlier for the State hospital, departing luxuriously in a sky-blue taxi.

There were but four of us there at the garage—Larry, Officers Williams and Peabody, and myself. Gene Hawkins, who had trailed the chief like a plump, disconsolate ghost during the greater part of the day, had departed bewilderedly for Vershire toward sunset, leav-ing the case in Larry's hands, and Officer Duncan had been relieved of duty at the gates and had accompanied the solicitor to town.

Our instructions, as Larry outlined them, were simple. We were to patrol the grounds in pairs, encircling the house completely, and were to be constantly on the alert for any marauders outside or any suspicious sights or sounds either without or within. We were to carry on in three-hour shifts, and the two not on duty were to nap in the rear seat of the limousine, ready for instant call in event of emergency.

"I tried to get a man in the house," Larry explained, "but old Peter told me they could take care of themselves. I suggested, too, that he might want me to call in outside help—a detective agency, or something of the sort—and he said it would cost too much! Of all the tight old skinflints—"

I shall never forget that nocturnal patrol, with the bright stars overhead and the lights of Vershire winking out one by one in the valley below. The night was gratefully cool after the torrid heat of the day, and the clean, fresh smell of the outdoors was all about us as we trod softly over the dew-wet grass, eyeing the dark bulk of the house apprehensively.

Larry and I had taken the first watch, from eight o'clock to eleven. When, after a fruitless three-hour vigil, we roused Peabody and Williams, the house was in utter darkness save for the single light in the cupola.

Though I had learned, since my arrival at Fitch's Folly, that this light always burned from sunset to sunrise, there was something eerie and disquieting about the tiny pinpoint of brilliance atop the sprawling bulk of the huge house. It was almost like an eye looking steadily down upon you.

I was bone-tired, but sleep would not come. Curled in one corner of the rear seat, I lay listening to Larry's regular breathing.

Somewhere out there in the darkness atop the mountain his two aids were carrying on. Queer that I could hear nothing of them. Queer that I could hear nothing . . .

I was in a burning building—bedridden, paralyzed. The flames were creeping slowly, inexorably toward me. I screamed at the top of my smoke-filled lungs, but no aid came . . .

The timbers beneath the floor were burning away. They snapped in a shower of stinging sparks. My bed, tilting, slid slowly toward the flaming inferno below . . .

I awoke with the cry of "Fire!" in my ears. For an instant I believed it a trailing echo of my nightmare.

Then, at the sound of pounding feet, I scrambled frantically from the limousine and stumbled out of the garage as Williams came hammering across the lawn. Behind him I could see, obscuring the starlit sky, a mounting pillar of ruddy smoke.

"Fire!" he panted. "Fire! It's the gardener's cottage!"

CHAPTER IX
TORCH MURDER

My thoughts galloped madly as I raced with Larry toward the cottage. Had George and Margery returned from their visit to Wenty? Was their tiny home empty, or had they been trapped and incinerated?

As we burst over the brow of the slope I breathed a sigh of relief. Outside the blazing building, their grotesque figures clear-cut against the flames, stood George, an old-fashioned nightshirt flapping about his thin calves, and his wife, with a wrapper hastily thrown about her stocky shoulders. It was obvious that they had retired before the blaze broke out, and had escaped, as the press cliché goes, scantily clad.

Of Peabody, however, there was no sign. I had ample time to envision him within the burning building before he appeared from the other side of the cottage. Behind him he dragged a garden hose from which he was directing a wabbly stream upon the flames, at the same time alternately bawling "Fire!" and "Help!" at the top of his lungs.

The fire at the cottage, I saw at once, was of no such proportions as the conflagration which two nights earlier had destroyed the barn. As I arrived at the scene I became aware that, although the east side of the building was blazing briskly, there seemed to be no fire in the interior.

The hose, by good fortune, was attached to a sillcock at the southwest corner of the cottage, well out of reach of the blaze. The pressure was good, the windmill having replenished the storage tank, but the flames, eating stubbornly into the weather-worn woodwork, were gaining ground despite Peabody's best efforts.

My cheeks stiffening in their familiar mask of fear, I stood watching spellbound. It was not until the flames had eaten through the dry shingles of the roof and were beginning to drop blazing embers within that the first drop of rain fell.

Tilting my face upward in surprise, I was almost blinded by a vivid flash of lightning. Until that moment I had not realized that the stars had been obscured and that the wind had suddenly risen. Now, drenched without warning by a sudden spatter of raindrops, I realized that a timely thundershower had arrived to lend its aid in extinguishing the blaze.

Within ten minutes the final flicker of fire had given way to smoking embers under the lashing sheets of rain, with able assistance from Peabody's hose. Then, without warning once more, the downpour abruptly abated, though lightning still played incessantly about the mountain top, illuminating the unreal scene. The temperature had dropped sharply, and I found myself soaked, shivering, and chilled to the bone.

Long before this the cottage was ringed by a sprinkling of spectators, their white faces ghastly in the lightning's glare. Larry, however, I noted, was not among them. He did not reappear until after Fire Chief Abel Stillwater and his retinue—late, as usual—had come roaring up the mountain, surveyed the scene disgustedly, and made their departure as unostentatiously as possible.

When I first saw him he was questioning George and Margery, who seemed scarcely to have moved from the spot where I had first seen them. I approached with undisguised curiosity.

"What time did you two get home?" Larry was asking, holding a brilliant beam focused upon their faces.

"About midnight, Chief," replied George gloomily. "Your man Williams saw us when we came in."

"How soon did you go to bed?"

"Right away. We were dog-tired."

"What roused you?"

"I smelled smoke," broke in Margery defiantly. "I punched George in the ribs, but he just grunted and turned over. I was just dozing off myself when I smelled it again, stronger'n ever. So I got up and looked out, and I saw the fire outside. I yelled at George, and we ran out—"

"Was there any sign of fire when you got home?"

"No."

"Or when you retired?"

"No."

Larry paused, switching the beam of his torch from one pallid countenance to the other.

"Did you see Wenty at the hospital?" he resumed.

"Yes," said Margery after a barely perceptible hesitation.

"What did he say?"

Margery hesitated again, her black eyes roving furtively. She had already opened her mouth when her husband's gloomy headshake forestalled her.

"I've told her there's no use lyin'," he said. "Fact is, Chief—we didn't see him at all!"

"Didn't see him?"

"No."

"Why not?"

"We couldn't."

"Oh, for God's sake, talk sense! crackled Larry. "Why couldn't you see him?"

George's characteristic stoop seemed to grow more pronounced, and his doglike eyes more hopeless.

"He'd got away," he said in a low tone.

"Got away?" gaped Larry.

"Yes."

"You mean—escaped?"

The gardener nodded somberly.

"What time?"

"He'd skipped just before we got there," amplified George. "They hunted inside the hospital for quite awhile—they swore he couldn't have got through the gates, and they thought he was hidin' somewhere. We waited and waited, but it didn't do no good. But just before we left, they got track of him. He'd bribed one of the guards—God knows how or what with—and he'd got outside and got into a car. And when we left, they'd traced the car as far as Campton."

I felt myself go cold with a chill due not alone to my water-soaked clothing. For Campton, I knew, was only ten miles distant.

Had Wenty, somehow mysteriously spirited back to Vershire, re-turned to Fitch's Folly to set fire to the cottage in which his parents slept? And if so, why? And how?

I edged involuntarily closer as Larry resumed his interrogation.

"Did you see him after you got back here tonight?" he demanded.

"We did not!" rapped out Margery.

Larry, ignoring her, turned his torch on her husband. George shook his grizzled head dully.

"No, Chief," he said. "We looked around a little, but we didn't see nothin' of him. If he did come back here, it wa'n't to the cottage."

I shivered as Larry, biting his lip, sent the powerful beam of his flashlight stabbing erratic circles through the darkness about us.

What if somewhere there on the lonely mountain top lurked Wenty, his deranged brain prompting him to hideous, unthinkable atrocities? What if—

The beam came to rest on a can beside the charred wall of the cottage. Larry, moving with swift strides, bent above it.

"I thought so!" he muttered.

"What is it?" I asked.

"Kerosene!" said Larry.

He lifted his voice in the darkness.

"Williams!" he called.

"Here, Chief!" came Williams' reply from somewhere behind me.

"Did you check up on everyone as I told you?"

"Yes, Chief! Everybody's here but—"

"All right!" cut in Larry hastily. "Now I want you and Peabody to take them up to the house—I want to talk to them a little later. Put them in the library and keep them there till I come."

"O. K., Chief."

Larry spoke no word until the scene of the fire was deserted by all but ourselves. Then, turning toward me, he thrust an extra torch into my reluctant hand.

"Come on, Bill," he said.

"Where?"

"In here," said Larry grimly, gesturing toward the cottage. "I've got a pretty good idea what we'll find in here—but I'm going to make sure."

My nerves crawled uncontrollably as I followed him into the half-burned building. Its walls were still standing, but part of the roof had fallen in, and the acrid odor of charred, water-soaked wood brought me to the verge of nausea.

Larry, picking his way carefully over a beam that had fallen athwart the open door, stood in the center of the tiny living room, flashing his torch in all directions. But the three rooms on the ground floor, we found, were empty, as were the two on the second floor, reached by a hazardous climb up the half-burned staircase.

Back once more in the living room, Larry stood frowning in perplexity.

"Any cellar under here?" he demanded.

"Not that I know of."

"Then where can it be?"

"What?" I queried shakily.

I do not know why I asked that. It seemed to me, even before the beam of his flashlight focused upon a tall cupboard in one corner, that I knew.

I stood stiffly, my hands clenched, as he moved slowly toward it, extended his hand, and gently released the catch on the door. The next instant I leaped backward as a body toppled forward into the room.

It lay face upward on the floor in the light of Larry's torch. Its blonde hair was dabbled with blood, its faded blue eyes staring blankly at the ceiling.

It was that of Guy's widow, Martha Fitch!

Kneeling, Larry lifted the lifeless head, turning it gently toward the wall. At the base of the skull, clear in the beam of light, was a hideous, blood-clotted bruise.

Larry, his jaws clamped together, rose slowly to his feet.

"Wh-what are you going to do now?" I stammered.

"I'm going to call Doc Reefer and the undertaker. If the extension phone isn't burned out—"

The wires, miraculously, had escaped damage, and the night operator's response for once was prompt. Five minutes later, having completed all necessary arrangements, Larry hung up and began a restless prowl about the wrecked room. But after a brief survey he shook his head despairingly.

"The fire wasn't a complete success," he commented, "thanks to Peabody and the rain. But it did enough damage so that it's hopeless work looking for clues here."

Lowering himself to the edge of a chair, he bowed his dark head in his hands and fell to furrowing his scalp with his fingers. I stirred uneasily, imagining all sorts of hideous faces peering in at us through the cracked and smoke-grimed windows.

"How about the folks up at the house?" I asked at length.

"They'll keep," said Larry grimly. "I lost something once by not keeping an eye on it—remember? Well, I don't intend to do it again."

It was not until Doc Reefer and the undertaker had come and gone that he made his departure, leaving me to stand guard.

"I'll send Peabody down to relieve you," he said. "Come up to the house as soon as he gets here."

My nerves, save for my fire phobia, are normally steady, and I had seen too much service in France to be unbalanced by sudden death. But my solitary vigil there in the half-burned cottage, with the odor of fire still strong in my nostrils and a killer loose somewhere in the darkness on the mountain top, was as hideous a quarter hour as I have ever spent. I am not ashamed to admit that, once relieved by the stocky and stolid Peabody, I ran most of the way to the house, arriving sadly out of breath and nursing a bad case of the jitters.

Williams, on guard at the library door, admitted me with a nod. Beyond him I saw Larry, standing behind the desk, sweeping the circle before him with his hard black eyes like an avenging judge.

Patty and Gilbert were side by side on the window seat, their hands linked together, their faces white and shocked. Peter Fitch, his tousled mop of white hair more untidy than ever, sat shriveled and shrunken in one corner, his eyes doggedly fixed on the floor. His grenadier spouse, defiantly erect, was reaching out a hand to pat the shoulder of her half-sister, who was crying quietly into a lace-bordered handkerchief. Ruth, her vivid, pointed face depicting frank dismay, stood just within the door, flanked on one side by Karl and on the other by Margery and George, who had somehow made themselves slightly more presentable.

It was obvious, even before I heard Larry speak, that his inquiry was making little progress, and his first words furnished confirmation.

"So that's your story, is it?" he said harshly. "Every last one of you sound asleep—didn't see anything or hear anything till the fire broke out, eh?"

Sleep-soaked eyes lifted torpidly to his challenging face, and a wordless murmur of assent reached my ears.

"Well, that's a help!" said the Vershire chief scathingly. "Because I don't mind telling you right now that unless I'm sadly mistaken, one of you is a liar—and before I get through, I'm going to find out who it is! And when I do—"

His dark eyes darted toward Williams, standing beside me in the doorway.

"Let's hear what you've got to say, Zenas!" he snapped. "You weren't sound asleep too, were you?"

Williams' round face grew several shades pinker, and he began to scuff his large feet on the timeworn carpet.

"'Course not!" he replied huskily. "Didn't I come running to wake you up as soon as I saw the—"

"Never mind that. Just what did you see and hear?"

"Not a G— not a cussed thing, Chief. Jesse and I patrolled the house, round and round, like you told us to. About an hour after you'd turned in, the taxi came up with George and his wife. They got out and went into the cottage. I was going down to peek in, but the lights went out right straight off."

Producing a handkerchief, he began to mop his perspiring forehead.

"And after that," he said, "there wasn't a sight nor a sound till the fire started!"

"Where were you when you first saw it?"

"We'd just come from around back of the house. Jesse spotted it and let out a yell, and we both legged it for the cottage as tight as we could go."

"You would!" said Larry bitterly.

"Huh?"

"Leaving the house here unguarded, of course?"

"Why should we guard the house?" demanded Williams truculently. "The fire was down at the cottage, wasn't it?"

Larry made a gesture of despair.

"And then what?" he demanded.

Williams scratched his head meditatively.

"Well, the fire sure burned up awful fast," he said. "Before we could get down there, the whole side of the house was going. So Jesse grabbed the hose and I ran back to wake you and Bill up. George and his wife were out by the time we got there—"

"And you didn't see anyone around the cottage?"

"I didn't look," said Williams with ingenuous honesty.

"I suppose you thought it was spontaneous combustion!"

"Huh?"

"Never mind," said Larry wearily.

He cast a glance at his wrist watch. I followed suit, and my heavy-lidded eyes widened. I had not realized that it was nearly three o'clock.

"Almost morning," he said, smothering a yawn. "Well, I suppose you folks might as well go back to bed and get some sleep—if you can. Williams, you go out and sit on the front steps—and for God's sake keep your eyes and ears open!"

"Where are you going to be, Chief?"

"I'm going to be right in this house!" announced Larry grimly. "If anything more happens here tonight, I want to know about it!"

Wearily the dwellers at Fitch's Folly dragged themselves from the room. Larry, crossing to close the door behind them, turned to eye me as I slumped sleepily into a chair beside the desk.

"Well, Bill?" he said. "What do you make of it?"

I shook my head hopelessly.

"Wenty?" I hazarded.

"It's possible, of course. But somehow I can't see him as a homicidal maniac all of a sudden, after all these years. I wonder where he is now."

I cast an apprehensive glance into the darkness beyond the uncurtained window beside me.

"I wonder how he got out of the hospital," I retorted.

"So do I, Bill. I can't imagine George having guts to plan anything like that. If it was either of them, it was certainly Margery. And how she'd be able to work it—"

"You don't think either of them set fire to the cottage?"

"I doubt it. In fact, I doubt if they knew the body was there. And if they didn't—if they came back to that dark cottage at midnight and went ahead getting ready for bed, while all the time Martha Fitch was dead in the cupboard there in the living room—"

I found my forehead suddenly moist with sweat. A little shame-facedly I rubbed it dry with my crooked forearm.

"But why should she go to the cottage alone—Martha, I mean?" I asked. "To meet the Wolds when they came home? And how could she get there without being seen?"

Larry, leaning forward, lowered his voice.

"I'll tell you something, Bill," he said. "Martha Fitch, according to Doc Reefer, had probably been dead about five hours when he examined the body at two o'clock this morning. And if that is true, it means—"

"It means," I broke in excitedly, "that she was killed while you and I were patrolling the grounds!"

Larry, scowling blackly, nodded.

"That's just what it means!" he admitted.

"But I don't see how—"

"Oh, I suppose it would be easy enough for her to slip out when we were on the other side of the house—there's no moon, you know. If we only knew who she had a date with—"

"But if she was killed then," I objected, "how did it happen the cottage wasn't set afire until well after midnight?"

Larry's broad shoulders lifted in their characteristic shrug.

"Do you believe," I went on, "that it was the same one who burned the barn?"

Larry shrugged again.

"Of course," he said wearily, "it's possible the two aren't connected at all. And as for who did it—God knows! There's always Wenty to fall back on—not to mention Dinwiddie and the tramp and the pair that skipped from Vershire. For that matter, anyone could have sneaked up in the dark and sloshed a can of kerosene over the cottage and set fire to it and skipped without being seen. I'm going to try to trace the can in the morning, but I'm not banking on it."

He paused, drumming an impatient tattoo on the table.

"But all the same, Bill," he went on, "I can't get rid of the notion that this is, as you might say, an inside job. There's some sort of a pattern behind it all—a pattern that we haven't been able to study out—and I'll swear the Fitch family is in it. And when—"

He broke off, holding up his hand for silence. "What's that?" he whispered.

I had heard it, too—a soft, stealthy padding of feet in the hall outside. Despite the lateness of the hour, someone was still astir in the huge house—someone who, it was obvious, sought to avoid attention.

Like a flash Larry was out of his chair and was tiptoeing noiselessly across the carpet. I rose softly to my feet, ready for—I knew not what. The insane thought possessed my mind that the footsteps were those of Wenty the half-wit, creeping through the darkness in the corridor outside on God alone knew what ghastly errand.

Larry was within a yard of the door when the footsteps suddenly ceased. His fingers were closing on the knob when a stealthy hand tapped softly on the panel.

Holding his gun ready in his right hand, with his left he jerked the door open with a single swift motion.

The next instant we both stood gaping like a pair of zanies.

Just outside the door, her patrician face pale but determined, stood Alice Lodge. At first glance she appeared fully dressed, but a second hasty look showed me that she had removed her shoes!

CHAPTER X
FAMILY SKELETONS

Without a word she crossed the threshold, treading quietly in her stockinged feet. As Larry's flaccid grasp on the knob of the door relaxed she swung it softly shut, crossed to a chair in the corner, and seated herself primly, thin hands clasped decorously in her black silk lap.

My mouth, I feel certain, was still ajar as Larry, recovering his poise with an obvious effort, thrust his gun rather sheepishly back into its holster. Still staring, he returned to his chair behind the table and seated himself rather heavily upon it. But his words, when at last they came, showed no hint of his bewilderment.

"You wished to see me, Mrs. Lodge?" he asked.

The faded occupant of the chair in the corner leaned toward him, her mouse-gray eyes blinking nervously.

"Yes, Chief," she said, in a voice but a shade above a whisper.

"Is it something about the murders?" Larry prompted her after a moment of silence.

"Yes, Chief. But—but I do not wish my visit here to be known. May I ask you to move a little closer?"

Surprisingly Larry rose, crossed to the corner, and seated himself on the floor at her feet.

"Yes, Mrs. Lodge?" he prompted, looking up at her.

"I feel that you should know," she said simply, "who it was that aided Wentworth to make his escape. It was my brother-in-law."

Larry, leaning back, eyed her incredulously.

"Peter Fitch?" he cried.

"Not so loud, please. Yes, it was Peter. Or rather, it was Judge Manning. I heard him telling the Judge what he wanted over the telephone before he went down there yesterday afternoon."

Larry started to speak, then paused.

"At the time," Alice Lodge continued, "I did not feel it my duty to speak. But now, since Martha's death, I believe it right that you should know. You may use the information in any way that you deem advisable. I trust, however, that you will keep its source a secret."

I stood gaping at the amazing tableau—the prim little old lady, with her black silk and lace collar, sitting so quietly there in the corner as she uttered these astounding words; Larry Frost, squatted on the floor at her feet, looking up at her with what I could well imagine was utter disbelief.

"Are you sure of that, Mrs. Lodge?" he asked at length.

Alice Lodge drew herself up with dignity.

"I am not accustomed to having my veracity questioned," she said.

"I beg your pardon. I didn't intend to doubt your word. But—why should he do it?"

At the query, to my further bewilderment, her fine-lined countenance became suffused with color.

"He—he thinks a great deal of Wentworth," she answered in a low tone. "He has always refused to permit him to be placed in—to be taken away. I have not agreed with him, nor with Nellie; but, as you perhaps know, I have no voice in the matter. I believe—I have always believed—that he is capable of any crime—"

"Do you believe him responsible for the deaths here at Fitch's Folly?" broke in Larry.

"Frankly, I do. And if he is not found at once—I understand from George that he has escaped—I fear there will be more!"

With a decisive nod she pursed her thin lips and made as if to rise. Larry held up a restraining hand.

"One moment, Mrs. Lodge," he said. "Before you go, will you be good enough to tell me the exact nature of Peter Fitch's interest in Wenty?"

Once more the wave of color flooded her thin cheeks.

"That," she answered between stiff lips, "is strictly a family matter."

Larry, rising abruptly, towered above her, his eyes searching her face. I am certain that for the time they had both forgotten my presence.

"Mrs. Lodge," he said emphatically, "this is no time for family matters to take precedence over the interests of justice. Two mysterious murders have been committed here, apparently without motive. At such a time every scrap of information, whether public or private, is vital. If you wish to be of assistance, you will tell the truth without concealment."

He paused, his hard black eyes holding her fluttering gaze in an almost visible grip.

"Is Margery Wold Wenty's mother?" he asked.

"Yes."

"And his father?"

The faded widow's spinsterish cheeks were crimson. One thin hand crept uncertainly to her throat. Her dry lips moved, but no words came.

"And his father?" Larry repeated inexorably.

Twice Alice Lodge lifted her head defiantly, only to let it drop once more. When at length she spoke, it was in a voice so low that I had to strain my ears to catch her faltering words.

"Guy Fitch," she faltered, and burst unrestrainedly into tears.

I was to learn that Larry's suspicions had been strong from the start—had, indeed, existed before the fires at Fitch's Folly ever began. They were based, I discovered, on an old wives' tale of nearly three decades earlier—a tale still whispered slyly through the town and responsible for much of Vershire's resentment at the "stuck-up airs" of the millionaire clan.

But as for myself, Alice Lodge's astounding revelation of the skeleton in the Fitch closet left me speechless and almost gasping.

I listened in amazement as Larry's skillful questioning—now stern, now cajoling—dragged the story from her reluctant lips. It was, in essence, one of the oldest of stories—the wild, headstrong, moneyed youth who in his parents' eyes could do no wrong; the alluring, provocative maid; the inevitable moonlight night, with the added stimulus of liquor . . .

Alice Lodge hid her face in her hands as she told this part of the story.

"He was—drunk," she said, shuddering. "And he'd given her some—"

I have since seen a picture of Margery Roberts in her girlhood—a wild, gypsy-looking creature of undeniable charm. She was mentally normal then, if a trifle inclined to be, as it was called in her day, "fast." But from that impetuous night on the mountain top, even before the birth of her child, she had been unquestionably more than a trifle mad.

The rest of the tale is soon told—the hushing up of the affair by means of the Fitch fortune; the farmhand who was willing to marry her and give her child a name; the lifelong tenure of the Wolds at Fitch's Folly as a reward.

Small wonder, I now realized, that Peter Fitch had opposed any move to have his grandson "put away," or that he had connived at his escape. Small wonder, too, that I had seen a likeness between the half-witted youth and the almost equally eccentric millionaire.

The ruddy hues of dawn were gleaming through the eastern windows when Alice Lodge at length left the room, walking quietly in her stockinged feet. I thought her both a pathetic and a tragic figure as she departed softly, her gray-coifed head held high, her mouse-gray eyes staring unseeingly before her.

I said as much to Larry, who had crossed to close the door after her. But Larry had no room in his thoughts just then for pathos or for tragedy. His active brain was already at work fitting this fresh piece of information into the still imperfect pattern.

"Well, Bill," he said, ignoring my comment, "that explains a lot. But there's a lot more that it doesn't explain. Why should Wenty turn on Guy—or on Guy's wife—after all these years? Why, if it's Wenty old Peter's afraid of, should he go to work and get him released? And why should Mrs. Lodge volunteer all her information at this particular time?"

"She didn't volunteer it," I objected. "You dragged it out of her."

He appeared not to have heard me.

"It doesn't explain the robbery, nor the attack on your boss," he went on, half to himself. "It doesn't explain Dinwiddie. It doesn't explain Mrs. Lodge's sulks the day before the Fourth. It doesn't explain what became of Guy's clothes. It doesn't explain—"

"Well, what does?" I interrupted impatiently. "If you know of any theory that covers all those—"

"I don't, Bill. But I need one, and I need it bad. Somehow some of those things must fit together and make sense—but I'll be damned if I know how!"

We both jumped as another knock sounded at the door. For a moment I visioned the library as a potential scene of continuous confessions by culprits or near-culprits in the affair at Fitch's Folly.

As the door swung open, however, I saw that it was Alice Lodge again. Her features were unnaturally pale, I thought, but she still held herself proudly erect.

"I listened—outside the door," she said simply, closing it behind her. "I had not realized that my own conduct was seriously in question. Perhaps I should tell you what Nellie and I disagreed about two days ago. It was Wentworth."

"Wentworth?" echoed Larry blankly.

The little old lady nodded.

"I had insisted that he be sent away," she said. "I had seen him—I caught him torturing a chicken with a—with a knife. I was afraid. I told Nellie—"

"And what did she say?"

Alice Lodge's face was colorless, but her voice was still steady.

"Nellie told me," she said, "that if anyone were to be sent away, it should be me. She pointed out that I was less closely related to the family than—than Wentworth was. She reminded me that I was only here on sufferance—that I was in reality an object of charity—"

She lifted her lace handkerchief to her trembling lips, and two large tears rolled slowly down her withered cheeks. Then, without another word, she turned and went out, closing the door softly behind her.

Larry and I stood staring speculatively at each other.

"Well," I said finally, breaking a protracted silence, "what are you going to do with all this dope?"

Larry did not answer until he had opened the door and looked out. But the dusky hallway, this time at least, was empty. Our strange visitor had vanished, presumably to her room; at all events she was no longer eavesdropping.

"I'm going to keep it under my hat for now," said the Vershire police head. "And so are you, Bill—don't forget that! Later on, perhaps, we can make some use of it—but not until we can figure where it all fits in."

It was broad daylight when I let myself quietly out of the front door, and paused, grinning despite my weariness.

On the top step sat the plump figure of Officer Zenas Williams, lolling sidewise against one of the fluted Colonial pillars of the porch. The strain of the night's events had proved too much for him, and he was snoring rhythmically if not tunefully.

Lacking the heart to disturb him, I decided to leave that for Larry. On tiptoe I descended the steps and made my way toward the garage.

It was a glorious midsummer morning, with all traces of the night's brief shower erased from the sweeping arch of blue and gold above my head. There was not a soul, it seemed, astir; I was alone upon the mountain top, monarch of all I surveyed.

For a moment I felt exultant, uplifted, like the discoverer of a new world. But the next instant, catching over my shoulder a glimpse of the charred roof of the gardener's cottage, I descended abruptly to the terra firma of grim reality. The morning air seemed suddenly chill, the solitude somehow terrifying. I found myself more than glad to be back once more between the familiar walls of my own room.

I was deathly tired, but I felt no desire for sleep. Instead, my brain seemed abnormally alert and active. Seating myself by my window, I fell to jotting down a series of notes.

The paper is before me as I write this chronicle. It seems odd, looking back on it all, that I could have struck so many false scents along with the true.

For a time I strove vainly to map out the motive behind the two murders. Why, since it was Old Peter who had been in obvious fear of death, had the initial blows been struck at his son and daughter-in-law? Had these been aimed at him and missed? Or were they deliberately designed as a planned campaign of terrorism calculated to wear him down and render him easy prey?

Abandoning this fruitless speculation, I set myself to an intensive study of the possible sources of the old man's fear. My Federal post, it is true, had given me no experience of a criminal nature. But I had prided myself, before the prison term which had left me little faith in myself or in others, that I had possessed the gift of methodical and orderly reasoning from cause to effect.

Was Peter Fitch, then, afraid of his family, or of outsiders?

His rambling incoherences presupposed a plot by some member of his own household, but of this I felt none too certain. Surely I had seen no sign of such a plot since my entry into his service, save possibly Guy's inexplicable actions on the day of his death. Indeed, I knew of no motive, unless it were revolt from old Peter's iron rule or resentment at his parsimony.

Was he afraid of blackmail? And if so, by whom?

I thought of the Wolds, only to dismiss them from my mind. Of a certainty George and Margery were too sensible of their present good fortune to attempt to kill the goose that laid the golden eggs. As for Wenty, old Peter's solicitude—extending even to the planning of his escape—indicated his belief that he had nothing to fear from that quarter. And it was obvious that he knew nothing of Wenty's fantastic accusations.

Had Patty some secret hold on her grandfather, other than his apparent affection for her? Were she and Gilbert engaged in some nefarious design upon his wealth? Was it possible that Ruth Vale was somehow involved, either with them or otherwise?

I thought of kidnapping, but dismissed this also. If abduction were contemplated, why had old Peter not been carried off two nights earlier, instead of being bound, gagged, and left in his library?

Moreover, if the old man actually entertained such fears, would he not take greater precautions in guarding his person and his mountain home?

And in thinking of the robbery I thought at once (I do not know why) of Karl Litzler.

Karl, I knew, despite his customary stolidity, was at least outwardly devoted to his employer. But how, after all, could the house have been entered so easily without inside aid? Had Karl been in league with the mysterious nocturnal visitors? Or had the pair who robbed and attacked Peter Fitch been members of his household?

Witchcraft?

I set down the word with an irrepressible shudder.

Was the mad kink in Wenty's brain an inheritance from his grandfather, or from his mother? Did the half-wit, through blood ties or superstition, have some mysterious hold over the old man?

I recalled Margery Wold's wild black eyes, gleaming darkly through the black witchlocks above her white forehead. Had she or her son put some diabolical spell on Peter Fitch, placing him in fear of his life?

I sat staring down at my notes, realizing with growing discouragement that they consisted chiefly of questions. I lifted my eyes, and the sight which I saw drove all further speculation from my mind.

The window at which I sat faced northward, toward the ridge which I had traversed on the afternoon of the Fourth to find Wenty beneath the huge pine. Now, midway of the apple orchard, I glimpsed a figure flitting from tree to tree in furtive fashion.

But it was not the actions of the unknown prowler that riveted my attention. It was the fact that *he was wearing Guy Fitch's clothes!*

CHAPTER XI
TANGLED TRAILS

I strained my eyes through the yellow morning sunlight, believing at first glance that I must be mistaken. The prowler, in fact, was too far distant for identification. But I was willing to take oath that the gray golf knickers, with the red and gray stockings beneath, were the same that Guy Fitch had worn the day the barn went up in flames, and the same that I had found Wenty trying to burn beneath the tree.

Thrusting my notes hastily into my pocket, I hurried down the stairs and out toward the orchard. I felt certain that the skulking figure I had seen played some part in the Fitch's Folly mystery. And in this, I later learned, I was not mistaken, though no stretch of my imagination could have visioned the tragic role to be thrust upon it before the final curtain was rung down.

Whether I was too late in reaching the scene, or whether the prowler had seen me and taken alarm, I had no means of knowing. At all events, I found the orchard empty, nor did a hasty search of the bordering woodland reveal any trace of what I was almost tempted to believe had been an apparition.

Returning in ill humor toward the house, I found my gaze resting upon the lofty cupola, its octagonal roof gleaming in the morning sunlight. It occurred to me suddenly that from such a coign of vantage I might be able to spy out the direction taken by the fugitive.

Breaking into a run, I regained the house and sped on tiptoe up the staircase. The dwellers atop the mountain, rudely roused from their slumbers a few hours earlier, were apparently dormant, and I had no desire to disturb them.

I had more than half expected to see Larry as I entered, but he was nowhere visible. Later I learned that he had made his departure precipitately following a hurry call from Acting Chief Forbes in the village below.

My previous trips of exploration with Larry enabled me to go at once to the empty room at the end of the hallway, in the ceiling of which was the trapdoor leading to the cupola. Turning to the closet behind the door, I dragged forth a tall stepladder which I recalled having seen there. It was covered with dust and cobwebs, and had obviously been unused for ages.

Dusting it sketchily with my handkerchief, I ascended its rickety treads with caution, gripping the sides as I climbed. Then, bracing myself, I lifted my hands above my head and pushed upward against the trapdoor with all my strength. But although the section of ceiling creaked encouragingly, it resisted my utmost efforts and refused to budge.

I was about to descend, defeated, when a rustle sounded behind me. I swung about, nearly upsetting the ladder.

Nellie Fitch stood in the doorway, staring at me in amazement. A bright-flowered negligee thrown about her bony shoulders served only to accentuate the ugliness of her horse-like face, haggard and unlovely in the clear light of morning.

"What are you doing up there?" she demanded in a venomous whisper.

"I was trying to get into the cupola, Madam," I replied sulkily, hoping devoutly that I looked and sounded less foolish than I felt.

"What for?"

There seemed no object in trying to explain my actions to the wrathy grande dame.

"I wanted to see the view," I muttered.

Nellie Fitch did not move from the threshold. Her baleful gaze, fraught with suspicion, clung to my face as I climbed hastily down the stepladder. I could feel it boring into the back of my neck as I returned the ladder to the closet, from which I emerged sneezing and dusting my hands.

"The cupola room has been closed for years," she said acidly. "I believe that it is locked. Now, if you have finished, I would suggest that you return to your quarters and try to make yourself present-able."

I retired to my own room in disorder, finding her suggestion jus-tified when I saw in my mirror a broad black band of dirt across my forehead. As for the mysterious prowler, my encounter with Nellie Fitch had driven him temporarily from my mind.

It was nearly eight o'clock before Larry came tearing back up the hill. Somehow he had found time during his absence to bathe, shave, and don fresh linen. His dapper appearance, I realized regretfully, was in sharp contrast to my own bedraggled self.

He alighted from the car just outside the garage. I hurried down to meet him.

"Well, Bill," he said happily, "we've located Brown and Robinson!"

"Where?"

"The police picked them up down in Hartford. Those weren't the names they gave, naturally, but the descriptions tally. I'm sending Sheriff Vickery down to bring them back. He was tickled to death. He was feeling a little bit sore because he hadn't been called in on this case, and probably he's justified. But God knows, it's bad enough to have Gene around, without having Oscar, too!"

"When will he get back?"

"Not till tomorrow. He can't get a train south before noon."

I stood eyeing Larry's cheerful countenance dubiously.

"You don't figure," I asked, "that they had anything to do with last night's murder?"

The smile faded from Larry's face.

"No," he said, "I don't. That's impossible, of course. But at least it's a lead—the first real one we've had. And if we can get that angle of it cleared up, maybe we can make some progress on the others."

Abruptly I was reminded of my own experience that morning. Larry whistled softly when I told him.

"Are you positive they were Guy's clothes?" he demanded.

"Absolutely."

"But you couldn't tell who was wearing them?"

"No. It was too far—"

Larry, slamming shut the door of his car, set out briskly for the house.

"What are you going to do?" I asked, falling into step.

"Do? I'm going to get a bunch of firemen and Legionaires up here and go through these woods with a fine-toothed comb! If there's someone hiding up here on the mountain we'll soon find out who it is!"

Within an hour more than fifty special deputies were beating the circle of woodland surrounding Fitch's Folly. The search continued during the remainder of the day, and by evening had been extended well into the forest outside the wall marking the boundary of the estate.

The wholesale hunt, however, failed to turn up the mysterious skulker I had seen that morning dressed in Guy Fitch's clothes. Whether he had fled the mountain top in fright at my pursuit, or whether he had cleverly concealed himself from the searchers, we had no means of knowing.

A detachment of firemen did come upon a hideout beneath a narrow ledge which, though empty, showed signs of recent occupancy. At least one fire had been built there, while dried crusts of bread and some empty tin cans, including several of "canned heat," indicated that the unknown tenant had lacked for neither food nor drink.

Upon this semi-cave Larry set a guard. He admitted, however, that he had little hope of trapping anyone.

"Nobody'd be as dumb as all that," he said. "There's just a chance, of course, that he might try to sneak back there tonight, after the search has died down—"

"Who might?" I asked. "Wenty?"

"Maybe," said Larry cryptically.

Our conversation took place late in the afternoon, with the searchers still in full cry at the outer edges of the mountain estate. During the morning I had participated in the hunt, as had Larry. On my return at noon, however, completely worn out, I had thrown myself down on the bed in my stiflingly hot room above the garage and had fallen into an uneasy and restless slumber, from which I had just awakened.

The shock of the second death at Fitch's Folly seemed to have stunned the whole household. Through the blistering heat of the blazing July day they moved like pallid ghosts, speaking for the most part in monosyllables, gazing uneasily about them as if expecting to see death lurking in every corner. Nor, in view of the ghastly experiences through which we all had passed, was I inclined to blame them.

Peter Fitch, naturally enough, seemed the most seriously perturbed. I was present at a conference he had with Larry shortly after I awoke, heavy-eyed and irritable, from my nap.

"Don't you see, Mr. Fitch," Larry said earnestly, "that if we don't know what to expect, it's almost impossible for us to protect you? Why don't you tell us what you're afraid of?"

Peter Fitch, huddled in one of the big armchairs, shivered. Somehow, since Martha's murder, he seemed older and more shrunken. Even his cracked, high-pitched voice had lost some of its shrillness.

"I don't know, Chief!" he piped feebly. "I thought I did—but I don't! First Guy, and then Martha—and next it'll be me! If I could only be sure—"

His thin, fluty voice trailed off into silence. He sat staring vacantly, a wizened, pathetic figure for all his millions. Despite my dislike, I could not help feeling genuinely sorry for him.

"Wouldn't you feel safer if I got some outside help?" Larry asked. "I'm willing to admit I'm not doing much of a job so far. A good detective agency, now—"

Old Peter shook his white-thatched head forlornly.

"It wouldn't help, Chief," he said. "All the detective agencies in the world couldn't save me. I haven't long to live anyhow—and if it's coming, I suppose, it's bound to come."

His thin body was racked by a fit of coughing which brought tears to his slaty eyes. Larry's face reflected tacit sympathy.

"I assure you, Mr. Fitch," he said, "that we're doing everything possible to protect you people up here. But I hope you realize that your attitude places us under a severe handicap."

Old Peter nodded, wiping his eyes.

"I understand, Chief," he said, "Just do the best you can, that's all—just do the very best you can—"

Larry and I exchanged significant glances above his bowed head as another fit of coughing convulsed him. Then, by mutual agreement, we rose quietly and left the room.

"Looks like the old boy's mind is beginning to crack up," said Larry softly when we had gained the porch. "No use trying to get anything out of him, I'm afraid. Well, I've got to go downtown. Keep an eye open while I'm gone, will you, Bill?"

"What are you going downtown for?" I asked curiously.

"I'm going to play a hunch," said Larry, and legged it for his car.

I wandered aimlessly in the direction of the gardener's cottage, with no particular expectation of finding anyone at the charred ruins. As I reached the brow of the slope, therefore, I was startled to catch sight of George and Margery, sitting side by side on the rustic bench under the tree beside it.

Their heads were close together, and they were grinning delightedly at each other, like a pair of children sharing a secret. But at sight of me twin masks of gloom dropped over their faces, for all the world like a modernistic play.

With a mechanical gesture of greeting I passed on, more than a little puzzled by what I had seen. Had they, I wondered, at last gotten in touch with Wenty? Or did their delight originate in a deeper and more sinister source?

Lost in my thoughts, I paid little heed to the route my feet were following. It was not until the subdued sound of voices brought me to myself with a start that I found I had penetrated deeply into the virgin forest adorning the eastern slope of the mountain, and was, in fact, within a few rods of the boundary wall.

Upon the wall, oblivious of my approach, sat Patty and Gilbert. Their backs were toward me, their legs dangling down the far side of the wall, and they were holding hands in the approved tradition of honeymooners.

I was about to beat a retreat when Gilbert's first words, assailing my startled ears, caused me to crouch hastily behind a stunted spruce.

"Are you sure she really knows, Pats?" he asked.

Patty turned sharply toward him. Her face, stripped of its customary vivacity, was positively shrewish. Once more I was reminded forcibly of the strain of ruthlessness which ran through the family.

"Knows?" she repeated. "Of course she knows—how could she help it? I only wonder if she's told!"

"But what shall we do?"

"There's only one thing for us to do! If she tells what she knows—we'll tell what we know!"

Gilbert's next words, tinged with bitterness, marked perhaps the first step in his matrimonial disillusionment.

"And I thought she was your best friend!" he said.

"She is, dear! But don't you understand? She doesn't matter at all—compared to you! I'd sacrifice her any minute—for your sake! Oh, Gilbert—"

The next instant she was sobbing in his arms, his dark head bowed above her platinum locks.

Heartsick, I turned and strode blindly away along the wall, my thoughts in a turmoil. There could be but one interpretation of their dialogue, one person to whom it could refer.

And almost at once, rounding the trunk of a huge tree, I came upon that person.

Ruth Vale was seated on the pine needles, her trim legs crossed beneath her short sport skirt, her dark head bowed in her hands. Her shoulders were shaking convulsively, and though she made no sound I knew that she was crying.

CHAPTER XII
WATCHERS IN THE DARK

She looked up quickly, dabbing at her wet eyes with her handkerchief. Kneeling beside her, I put my arm about her slim shoulders.

"What is it, dear?" I whispered.

She shook her head without speaking, and laid a finger on her lips.

A faint crackling sounded in the woods behind me. I wheeled, peering around the trunk of the tree. But it was only Patty and Gilbert, who had descended from the wall and were making their way back up the wooded slope toward the house.

Not until they had passed completely out of earshot did Ruth relax. Then, turning, she buried her face blindly in my shirtfront and burst into racking sobs.

"What is it, Ruth?" I repeated, patting her shoulder.

"Did you—did you hear them?"

"Yes. What did they mean?"

"They meant—oh, it's too horrid! And to think that Patty—"

She lifted her head, biting her lower lip determinedly.

"I suppose I'm being silly and childish about it," she said, her voice once more under control. "I probably wouldn't act this way, if these fires and all hadn't keyed up my nerves. I suppose I ought to be sorry I overheard her, but I'm not. It's a good cure for too much faith in human nature!"

"But what did she mean by saying they'd tell what they knew about you?" I asked in bewilderment.

She faced me squarely, her dark eyes steady. "About me—and Guy," she said in a low tone.

"*Guy?*"

She flushed hotly, but her gaze did not waver.

"Oh, it's not what you think," she said, her words coming with a rush. "It happened two years ago, when Patty was in college. He used to visit her, of course, and he'd make it a point to call on me too—his daughter's favorite teacher, and all that sort of thing. I didn't think anything of it at first. I even went out to dinner with him a few times. I knew I shouldn't—the head was pretty strict about that sort of thing—but I couldn't see any harm in it.

"The last time he came he'd been drinking—I didn't know it until after we'd started. He took me to a roadhouse and bought some more liquor there. He insisted on a private room, and I had to give in to avoid a scene.

"Then—"

Her low voice faltered, broke.

"Oh, it was beastly!" she whispered. "He locked the door and tried to attack me. I had to beat him off with a chair. By the time they'd broken in the door, I'd stunned him—knocked him unconscious! I thought he was dead—and I didn't care! I was glad!

"It was all hushed up somehow—the Fitch money, of course. He came the next day to apologize—he fairly got on his knees to me—and after that he was always absolutely decent. But Patty got a hint of it somehow, and one day she came to me and asked me what it was all about.

"Perhaps I shouldn't have told her the whole story, but I did. She was old enough to understand—she knew her father pretty well, after all. She broke down and cried, and asked me not to let it make any difference in our friendship—and for that matter, it never has. But now—"

All trace of tears had vanished from her eyes. A dark flame burned in their resentful depths.

"Don't you see?" she cried. "Patty's remembered that I overheard the quarrel that night, and they're desperate! If they do tell, and the police start raking over a dirty mess like that—"

"But that's no motive for murder!" I expostulated. "Because Guy involved you in a scandal two years ago—"

"That's just it—the scandal! Think what the tabloids would do with a story like that! Do you suppose I could go back to teaching this fall? Do you suppose I could be a councilor at a girls' camp? Do you suppose a dozen persons who read it—even if they printed the actual facts, which they wouldn't—would believe my side of it?"

I was silent, seeking in vain for words of encouragement. The picture that she painted was all too cruelly true. No college could afford to have a member of its faculty linked in such sordid fashion with a murder mystery as widely publicized as the affair at Fitch's Folly had now become.

Her own guilt or innocence would not matter. The mere fact that the story had appeared in print would be enough to damn her.

"Listen, Ruth," I said finally. "I'd get Patty alone, if I were you, and lay your cards on the table. Tell her that you overheard the quarrel, and that you overheard them today. Tell her that you believe Gilbert innocent—that you haven't said anything to the police, and don't intend to. She's lost her head completely, worrying about his arrest. If you can assure her that he is in no danger through you—"

"Then you don't think he's guilty?"

"I don't *think* so, no," I said slowly. "But that's not the question right now. I'm thinking how you can best protect yourself for the present. And, of course, it may develop that you need never tell the police at all."

But when she had gone, threading her way among the trunks of the trees thrusting upward from the mountain side, I sat staring thoughtfully after her, my brain beset by renewed misgivings.

Had I, after all, advised her in the best interests of justice? Or had I once more allowed my increasing infatuation to sway my better judgment?

I had not been able to settle the question to my own satisfaction when, rather tardily, I made my own way back to the house. It was nearing dusk, but the heat of the day had not in the least abated, and the air was oven-like and breathless.

As I came within sight of the house I looked up sharply at the sound of my name. At her window on the second floor stood Nellie Fitch, screeching at the top of her aged lungs.

I burst into a run, cursing myself for my carelessness. Larry had warned me to be alert, and I had failed. If anything had happened in my absence—

"What is it, Madam?" I shouted as I neared the house.

"The car!" she yelled back.

"What car?"

"The limousine! Bring it around at once! Hurry, you slowpoke!"

With mingled relief and resentment I altered my course in the direction of the garage, not daring to stop and ask what had occurred. The habits of even a few years, I discovered, are difficult to break. My reaction, I realized, was that of the typical menial, born and schooled to a lifetime of servitude.

My resentment mounted as I climbed hurriedly into the driver's seat, and I cursed myself wholeheartedly for my meekness. Then and there I solemnly vowed that, once the affair at Fitch's Folly had been settled, I would shatter the shackles of indifference which bound me to my present lowly state. Though the Federal service might still be closed to me, I now realized that lack of incentive alone had kept me from finding other work outside the servant class to which I now belonged.

I did not realize, oddly enough, the part which Ruth Vale played in my sudden determination to get out of my rut.

Nellie Fitch, attired for travel and carrying a small overnight bag, was fidgeting impatiently beneath the porte-cochère as I brought the car around with a flourish. She glared angrily at me as I sprang out to open the rear door.

"I've been ringing the garage for an hour!" she said, her voice crackling with rage. "Pity you couldn't stay on the job instead of mooning around in the woods with that Vale girl! What do you think we pay you for, anyway—so we can drive our own cars when we want to go anywhere?"

I felt the blood creeping up under my collar. "Where to, Madam?" I asked stiffly.

"The station, stupid! I'm catching the train for New York! My sister's been hurt—I just got a telegram from her husband! Hurry up— don't stand there gaping like an idiot!"

I paused, prey to sudden suspicion. I had no proof that there had actually been a telegram. What if this move on her part proved to be a ruse to escape?

I longed for Larry, but he was nowhere visible. What would he say when he found that one of the potential suspects in the case had been driven to the railway station by his deputy?

"Pardon me, Madam," I said firmly. "May I see the telegram?"

Nellie Fitch looked for a moment as if she were about to explode. Then, with a harsh, unpleasant bark of a laugh, she snapped open her handbag.

"So you think I'm running away, do you?" she sneered. "Here—read that! And I might add, since you're so worried about it, that your wonderful Chief Frost knows all about it and has given me his permission to go!"

My face flushed as I scanned the yellow slip she had thrust into my hand. Its appearance was undeniably authentic, and its message was imperative.

GRACE BADLY HURT IN MOTOR
CAR CRASH COME AT ONCE VINCENT

"That's Grace's husband," explained Nellie Fitch tartly. "His name's Vinson, but the telegraph company never gets anything right anyway. Now if you'll be good enough to get in there and drive, it's possible we may still be in time to catch the train."

Nettled, I slammed shut the door and started the car with a jump. My exasperation expressed itself further in a dizzy dash down the winding road which would have reduced the average woman to a state of collapse. But Nellie Fitch, unruffled, gave me a grim nod as she descended from the car with the southbound train already whistling for Baldwin's crossing a mile up the valley.

"Good time, Perley," she said approvingly. "Now hurry in and get my ticket—there's no sense in taking a sleeper for this trip."

Three minutes later the train pulled out with a clank of couplings and a shower of sparks. Nellie Fitch, sitting bolt upright, was clearly visible through the window of the last coach.

I stood staring at the red lights until they winked out of sight in the dusk. I was recalling, as I stood there, the departure of Dinwiddie on the same train three nights earlier, and the unsolved mystery of his subsequent disappearance. I found myself wondering rather morbidly if old Peter's wife might not vanish likewise.

Sighing wearily, I turned back to the waiting limousine, positive that she had remained aboard the train, whatever Dinwiddie might or might not have done. Tonight, instead of dallying downtown, I pointed my radiator at once for Fitch's Folly. I could still recall too clearly the night on which the barn had blazed vividly skyward while I sat in the Vershire Café sipping at my glass of ale.

As I drove up Main Street I cast an apprehensive glance at the tiny buildings, a mile away and aloft, silhouetted against the gleaming western sky. But this night no flare of flames, no pillar of smoke, met my eye; the roofs, serene and peaceful, seemed fairly to float on a shimmering sea of gold. It was all but dark before I reached Fitch's Folly. Larry hailed me as I drove up.

"Get your car in the garage and come back here!" he commanded curtly.

Returning, I found him pacing nervously up and down on the lawn just across the graveled drive in front of the house, with his two assistants standing stolidly by. His muscular fingers gripped my arm as he drew us together.

"Listen, Bill!" he said, his low voice tense. "I've got twenty firemen patrolling the woods along the wall. They're all deputized, and they're all armed. I suspect Fitch's Folly will be a tough place to get at from the outside tonight. But if anyone does sneak through—have you got a gun and a flashlight?"

"Up in my room," I nodded.

"Go and get them, then. You and I are going to take care of the grounds tonight—the second line of defense, so to speak. No—wait a minute! You might as well hear the rest of this, so you'll know what's going on."

He turned to Williams and Peabody, twin bulks of blue in the dusk.

"Zenas," he said, "I'm putting you on the second floor tonight. Jesse, you're guarding the ground floor. Get some chairs, if you want, to put in the halls—but don't go to sleep! Keep your eyes and ears open every minute! And if you see or hear anything suspicious—"

"I thought the old so-and-so didn't want anybody inside the house," mumbled Peabody, with an uneasy glance at the lighted windows beyond the driveway.

"I don't care what he wants!" snapped Larry. "I'm running this show tonight—and he'll take it and like it!"

"Who's sleeping on the second floor?" asked Williams, with unusual acumen.

"Everyone except the servants—God knows why, except that's the way the house is laid out. The old man's room is on the southeast corner, and his wife's opposite, on the southwest. All the others are on the west side—first Patty's and Gilbert's, then Miss Vale's, and then Mrs. Lodge's. The other three rooms on this side are empty. And downstairs—"

He turned to Peabody, who was still eyeing the house uneasily.

"Downstairs," he repeated, "Karl Litzler's room is next to the butler's pantry—know where that is? All right. The Wolds are bunking in the room next to his, on the south end. There's no one else on the first floor. That all straight?"

Both officers nodded solemnly. Larry leaned toward them, smacking his fist into his palm with noiseless emphasis.

"Now get this, you two!" he said. "Don't either of you leave the house, no matter what happens—you stick right where you are! If anything breaks outside, there'll be plenty of us to take care of it! Understand?"

"O. K., Chief!" came the answering duet.

"You'd better take your stations right away, then. The lights in the halls will be left on, and don't go monkeying with the switches! Got plenty of cigarettes and matches? Got your guns and torches, both of you? Go ahead, then!"

The front door swung shut behind the lumbering pair. Larry turned to me, grinning wryly.

"Regular wet nurse, eh?" he said. "Well, that's what those two need! Get your gun and flashlight now, Bill. You take the back of the house, and I'll take the front. Keep your eyes and ears open—I don't need to tell you that. Sleepy?"

I was, but I dared not admit it.

"How about you?" I countered. "I'll bet you didn't get even a nap today!"

"You win," nodded Larry. "But I'd go without sleep for a week if I could lay my hands on the bird that's pulling this stuff off up here!"

Getting my gun—a World War relic, but still serviceable—I thrust it with my flashlight into my pocket and made my way to the rear of the house. Here, seating myself on the top step of the porch, I rested my weary back against the pillar of the railing and sat staring out into the darkness.

Although the sun had been set for more than an hour, there was no lessening of the deadly heat which during the day had enveloped the valley in a blistering blanket. Moreover, a hot, dry wind had sprung up with the sunset. It blew steadily from the westward, rustling the trees about me. An air of hushed expectancy seemed to envelop the mountain top. From afar, eerily thin, came the faint whistle of a locomotive.

Despite my best efforts I presently found myself drifting into a doze. Rousing, I fixed my eyes on a bright star just above the far horizon, only to find its beams exerting a hypnotic effect little short of mesmeric.

Shaking myself, I rose and tiptoed down the brick walk, turning to stare at the dark bulk of the house towering above me.

All windows on the first floor were in darkness, and all on the second floor save two. I tried to recall Larry's word picture of the second floor rooms, but without success. They were either Ruth's and Patty's, or Ruth's and Alice Lodge's, but which I could not be certain.

Both windows, as I watched, went dark almost simultaneously. The huge house was black from basement to ridgepole, save where the perpetual light burned in the cupola above.

Despite the heat, I found myself shivering a little as I retraced my steps. It would seem that Larry had provided for all possible contingencies, but for all that I felt none too secure.

My thoughts turned to the pair due to be returned to Vershire for questioning the following morning. If they were truly guilty of the robbery, as was at least strongly indicated, Larry's precautions appeared decidedly superfluous.

But if they were not . . .

I drifted once more into a semi-doze, from which I was roused by a faint rustling toward the trees at my right, just beyond the sunken garden.

I sat erect with a start, straining my ears. It might, of course, have been a dream, or the noise of the wind in the trees, but it had sounded like a stealthy footfall in the grass.

The noise, however, was not repeated, and at length I relaxed once more. This time, however, I was doubly determined to keep awake, and when I felt my senses slipping I rose and walked doggedly up and down on the grass beside the path.

It occurred to me to wonder how Larry's vigil fared. With a final glance about me I tiptoed noiselessly toward the front of the house.

The beam of a torch struck me full in the face as I rounded the corner. Blinded, I fumbled for my gun, only to relax for a moment as Larry's voice said softly:

"Easy, Bill! How's it going?"

"Tough!" I whispered back as his torch clicked off. "I'm dead on my feet! How about you?"

"Ditto," said Larry, moving nearer. "All quiet?"

I thought of the rustle I had heard, but decided it was not worth mentioning. After all, I had probably imagined or dreamed it.

"Too quiet," I said, yawning. "I've got to keep on the move, or I won't hear anything till morning. What time is it?"

Larry consulted the luminous dial of his wrist watch.

"Eleven-fifty," he said. "Better be getting back, Bill. This may be all wasted effort, but I can't afford to miss a trick."

Reluctantly I returned to the rear of the house, finding all still dark and silent. The hot west wind, far from diminishing, was growing steadily stronger, and two branches in the blackness above my head had set up a persistent, monotonous groaning which kept my teeth on edge.

It must have been past midnight when I started up suddenly, bathed in perspiration, with a cry ringing in my ears. Was it a dream, a nightmare? No, for it came again, faint and far off, borne by the breeze—a woman's cry!

"*Fire! Fire!*"

I stood leaning forward—tense, staring. Were my heavy eyes playing me tricks?

The next instant, yelling wildly, I was running down the path and through the tall grass of the field beyond. For I had seen a flicker of flame, licking its way up the trunk of a tall spruce near the western wall, burst at its top in a shower of sparks like a swarm of deadly fireflies!

CHAPTER XIII
BLACK MAGIC

Behind me answering shouts echoed from Fitch's Folly. Looking back as I ran, I could see its windows coming alive with lights. Dark figures had begun to trail me across the field as I plunged into the woods, following as best I could the winding path which led to the home of Della Dole beyond the western wall.

The fire, I later learned, had started just inside the wall, not more than a stone's throw from the Dole home. Now, halfway down the path, I halted, terrified, as I came suddenly upon the forefront of the conflagration.

In the brief period since I had seen the fire from Fitch's Folly it had grown and gained ground almost beyond belief. Sparks were dropping crazily through the branches dozens of yards ahead of the main body of the blaze, starting fresh fires which were speedily fanned by the high wind to menacing proportions.

As I stood there, shivering, trying to force myself forward, I was joined by a half dozen firemen, their grimed faces dripping with perspiration. They were retreating slowly before the spread of the flames, now advancing along a broad front upon Fitch's Folly.

"What are you waiting for?" I demanded. "Why don't you do something?"

They eyed me stolidly without speaking. It was not until I had repeated my question that a spokesman vouchsafed reply.

"Nothing to do, feller," he said gruffly. "Take a couple hundred men to stop one like that—and even then, with the wind and all, we'd have our hands full. All we can do is to watch the edges and let it burn itself out. We can get it when it gets into the field, and with this wind it can't go any other place."

"But a backfire—"

For answer he pointed aloft. Looking up, I saw a huge pine bough, detaching itself from its parent trunk, borne blazing eastward out of sight, eddying giddily in the superheated air currents like a Fourth of July balloon.

"Backfire, hell!" he said, and spat scornfully on the ground.

Newcomers continued to join our group as we retreated. I had no idea how many spectators had been attracted to the scene, but it seemed, from the number of figures flitting about, that they must include not only the twenty firemen and the dwellers at Fitch's Folly, but half the population of Vershire as well. I remember particularly the spectacle of Karl, his torso nude, a pair of trousers belted about his waist, staring at the flames in terrified fascination.

We were shortly forced into the open field as the wind-borne flames burst from the edge of the woods with a leaping roar. At once we found plenty to do in beating out the grass fires which sprang up by the score in all directions.

Someone had had the forethought to bring two axes from the wood-shed which old Herkimer had used, and these were shortly supplemented by additional axes from the fire apparatus which stood chugging away uselessly at a safe distance. Some of these were used to cut branches for the beaters, and others to fell blazing trees along the sides of the straight swath cut through the forest from wall to clearing.

Gradually the lurid glare faded, the overpowering heat lessened. And then, of a sudden, I heard Larry's sharp voice behind me.

"What in hell are you doing down here, Zenas?"

I wheeled, to see Williams belaboring a blaze with a branch. He straightened, red-faced and wheezing.

"Fightin' the fire!" he panted.

"Didn't I tell you to stay on duty inside the house, no matter what happened?"

"Well, gee whiz, Chief! They don't need anybody back there now! Everybody's down here at the fire! So Jesse and I—"

"Peabody, too?"

"Sure! We figured we'd be more help down here than we'd be—"

Larry spun sharply toward me. His face, despite the ruddy reflection of the dying fire, looked dead white.

"Come on, Bill!" he commanded. "Back to the house—quick!"

Panic gripped me as I raced back across the field. Larry, beside me, was cursing Williams and Peabody beneath his breath.

Before us loomed Fitch's Folly—forbidding, deserted, sinister. And my heart sank suddenly as I noted that the house, save for the single light in the cupola, was in utter darkness!

With redoubled speed we sprinted up the slope, rounded the corner of the building, and halted suddenly, aghast.

The house itself, viewed from its eastern side, stood silent, deserted, and to all appearances unmolested. But beyond it, along the ridge to the south, fierce flames were leaping skyward.

"The windmill!" gasped Larry.

The tiny shack beneath the straddling structure was ablaze, and tongues of flame were licking upward about its steel skeleton, gaunt against the glare. Red light flickered from the blades of the huge fan above, spinning crazily under the impact of the fierce, hot wind.

Larry started along the ridge on the dead run. He waved me back as I sought to follow.

"The house!" he panted, pointing. "See if everything's—all right!"

My heart hammered as I approached in considerable trepidation, which did not lessen as I entered the open front door to find the entire house in darkness, with even the hall lights extinguished.

I fumbled for my flashlight, only to discover it missing. Apparently it had jolted from my pocket as I ran down across the field.

My only thought was of Ruth as I groped my way toward the staircase and stumbled haltingly upward. I had just remembered that I had not seen her at the fire.

What if some evil had overtaken her, there in the pitch-black house? What if—

Reaching the upper hall, I started toward what I thought was her room. My foot struck something soft, and I all but tripped and fell headlong.

Recovering, I knelt and extended an exploring hand. A deadly chill gripped me as my fingers touched a face. It felt cold and lifeless, like the face of a corpse!

I all but obeyed the impulse to let out a yell of sheer terror and bolt headlong down the dark stairway and out into the warm starlight outside. Instead, I crouched cringing in the blackness, my teeth chattering with pure fear.

What if the murderer lurked there in the darkness—perhaps actually within reach? What if the next instant my own body lay stretched beside the one at my feet?

Clenching my chattering teeth, I got a grip on myself and extended my hand once more, passing my fingers over the unseen face. It felt cool, but not clammy, and its delicate skin texture revealed no trace of a beard.

Suddenly I knew—I cannot tell how—whose body lay at my feet. Leaping up, I fumbled frantically for the light switch which I had at last remembered. It seemed ages before it spun and clicked beneath my frenzied fingers.

I turned, blinking in the sudden glare, to find my worst fears realized.

On the floor at my feet lay Ruth, her white face tilted back along one outflung arm, her bare legs twisted awkwardly beneath her dressing gown. She lay like one dead, and the chalky pallor of her features intensified my belief.

Dry-lipped and heartsick, I knelt beside her. And as I did, I saw, with a throb of relief, the slow rise and fall of her bosom. She was not dead, but merely unconscious!

I lifted the dark head gently to my lap. Beneath the blue-black close-cropped hair at the nape of the smooth neck I could feel an ugly lump.

Had she been struck down and left for dead by someone in the huge, horror-haunted house? Or had she sustained the injury in a fall while hurrying along the hall in the darkness?

But Ruth's first halting words, when she opened her eyes a moment later, left me in no doubt.

She had been standing, she said, at the head of the stairs, debating whether to dress and go to the fire or to return to bed, when the hall lights had suddenly been extinguished. As she had tried, blinded by the blackness, to grope her way back to her room, she had heard the sound of a soft footfall. Before she could call for help her skull had exploded into swirling stars, and she remembered nothing more.

"And you didn't see who it was?" I asked, cradling her dark head gently as she lay there with closed eyes.

"No, Bill," she murmured.

"Who was in the house at the time?"

She passed her hand wearily over her white forehead.

"I don't remember," she said. "I thought everyone had gone down to the fire. They'd all been running up and down and shouting—"

"Had Gilbert gone?"

"I think so," she answered dreamily. "I seem to remember—Gilbert and Patty—"

Her voice trailed off into a whisper. She was still barely conscious, but apparently there had been no serious concussion. I shuddered to think what might have happened, had the blow fallen squarely or with greater force.

With a start I remembered Larry and the windmill fire. Agreeable as my present attitude and occupation might be, the grim task of finding the fiend of Fitch's Folly still remained.

Ruth's lids fluttered and lifted slowly. She lay looking up at me, her bright dark eyes wide with worry.

"What is it, Bill?" she asked. "Is something—is there something—"

"Are you able to walk, dear?" I asked.

Courageously she lifted her head, and with my aid was able to struggle to her feet. I passed my arm about her waist to lend support as she made her way slowly back down the corridor into her room, where she relaxed limply upon the bed.

Her eyes followed me as I peered beneath it, searched the closet, and even thrust my head out of the window to make sure no prowler lurked on the sill outside. She even smiled faintly as I crossed to the door.

"Ruth!" I said, turning.

"Yes, Bill?"

"Lock the door behind me—you'll be safe then. And don't let anyone in—no matter what happens—until I come back. Right?"

"Right."

I waited outside in the hall until I heard the bolt click home. Then, gripping my automatic, I made a hasty but thorough search of the entire second floor.

Door after door I thrust open, fearing to find I knew not what dread secrets within. But every room was empty, nor did any closet prove to contain a hidden assassin.

Once, yanking open a closet door, I started back at sight of a gaunt shape looming within. But a second glance showed it to be only the stepladder which I had sketchily dusted and attempted to use less than twenty-four hours earlier.

Completing my fruitless rounds, I descended the stairs, switched on the lights in the lower hall, and stood hesitating. Should I finish the search of the house, or should I go to Larry's aid?

I wheeled at the sound of footsteps hurrying across the broad porch outside. Larry, bursting in, stopped short at sight of me.

"Well, thank God!" he said explosively. "I was beginning to think they'd got you, too! Find anything wrong?"

Briefly I sketched my discoveries. Larry whistled softly.

"Knocked out, eh? Where is she now?"

"I told her to lock herself in her room."

"Good man!" commented Larry.

"But who set fire to the windmill?" I asked.

"I don't know, Bill. And I don't know why, either—but I'm going to find out pretty soon. It's practically out, and I'm having the fire department soak it down—"

Suddenly I found myself shaking uncontrollably.

"You mean," I said, articulating with difficulty, "you mean—you expect to find—"

Larry's jaw was firm, his dark face dour.

"I've given up expecting anything sane in this nightmare," he said. "But in view of what we've found after the other two fires—"

"Who?"

The monosyllable burst irrepressibly from my stiff lips. Larry laid a firm hand on my shoulders.

"I don't know that either, Bill," he said soberly. "I haven't an idea. I've guessed wrong on this business once already—"

He shook his head impatiently, like a dog pestered by a persistent, buzzing fly.

"Right now, before anyone gets back," he said, "we'll finish the job of searching the house. You take the rooms on that side, and I'll take these—"

"But the fire—the windmill! Hadn't we—shouldn't you—"

"Williams and Peabody are on guard," said Larry, his tones grim. "And I think, after what I just told them, they'll stick till I get back—this time! Of all the peanut-headed, sponge-bellied—"

His voice soared in lurid invective which carried me back over nearly two decades to my brief Army career. I had never credited him with such fluency.

"Believe me, they could walk under a dachshund with their helmets on right now!" he concluded following a final outburst. "When I think where we might be, if they hadn't gone chasing off like a pair of eight-year-olds to a bonfire—"

He broke off with a shrug of resignation.

"Oh, well—it can't be helped now," he said. "Let's get going—and for God's sake be careful!"

"What do you expect to find?" I asked.

Larry gave a grimace of disgust.

"Nothing, probably!" he snapped. "That's all we've ever found so far when we started looking for something. But that's no excuse for taking chances. Sooner or later we'll have a stroke of dumb luck and find something!"

My side of the house included the huge library, the even more spacious living room or parlor, the smaller room adjoining which was Karl's, and the still smaller room at the rear temporarily occupied by the Wolds. With drawn revolver I moved rapidly from room to room, switching on lights as I went.

But on the first floor, as on the second, I drew a complete blank. There were no blood-stained corpses, no hidden assassins, no startling sights of any sort—merely the rooms themselves, bare and empty under the glare of the lights.

It was not until I was about to leave the fourth room—that of George and Margery—that I came upon something which gave me a decided shock.

I had almost passed it by, half hidden in the litter of belongings that Margery had salvaged from the half-burned cottage. Now, slowly, I retraced my steps, staring incredulously at the tiny object which had caught my eye.

It was a miniature figure crudely modeled from wax, completely with arms and legs—a hideous, misshapen figurine, twisted and faceless.

And through the center of the ugly body, protruding at both front and rear, had been thrust a rusty needle!

CHAPTER XIV
CHECK-UP

I am not, I believe, ordinarily superstitious; my abject fear of fire was, I prided myself, my only weakness. But as I eyed the hideous wax image, pierced through and through with such unmistakable and deadly intent, I could not repress a shiver of sheer dread.

Here, indeed, was a new angle on the days of haggard horror through which we on the mountain top were passing. I had heard as a child, from the withered lips of the aunt who had brought me up, how witches in the olden days had sought thus to bring death by black magic to those they hated.

Did Margery herself, with her strain of madness, hold with such infamous practices? Had she fashioned this figure from wax with the avowed intent of bringing death?

And if so, to whom?

I do not know how long I stood there staring in fascination at my find. It was not until I heard Larry's voice in the kitchen beyond that I wrenched my gaze from the hideous sight.

Larry looked at me curiously as I appeared.

"You look as if you'd seen a ghost, Bill," he said. "What did you find?"

"Nothing," I said, a little hoarsely. This was no time, I felt, to tell him of the figurine, with more immediate problems clamoring for action.

"So did I," said Larry grimly. "Let's get outside, now, and check up—if we can! A sweet chance we've got, with half the population of Vershire milling around up here by now and everybody scattered all over the top of the mountain!"

He opened the rear door and threw it wide with a vicious yank. Dry-lipped, I followed him out into the night.

The hot wind was still blowing from the west, beating against my face like the heat from a giant furnace. The illusion was heightened by the acrid odor of smoke which assailed my nostrils from the fire in the forest at the far edge of the field. Only a dull glow was now visible, save where some blazing trunk still sent flames streaming skyward, with tiny black figures capering about it like demons in Hades.

Larry, his fists clenched, stood staring blackly down the slope.

"I'd give my right hand to know how that started!" he muttered. "You can't tell me it was any accident!"

"What do you mean?"

"Too damned opportune!"

"But why—"

"Never mind. We'll talk later. Let's go!"

Rounding the corner of the house, we came at once into full view of the spectral skeleton of the windmill tower, limned starkly against the starlit sky. There were no flames now—only a thick column of vapor rolling heavenward from the hissing embers, on which the valiant Vershire firemen were still squirting water from the replenished tank on the ridge.

A sizeable crowd clustered curiously about its foot. Pushing our way through, we found ourselves within the extemporized fire lines which members of the department, assisted by Williams and Peabody, had established.

Larry cast a single contemptuous glance at his two aides as he passed. Beyond them Chief Abel Stillwater, megaphone clamped to his thin lips, was directing the one-sided battle against the practically defunct fire demon.

"How soon will that be cool enough to dig into, Abel?" Larry demanded in a low tone.

Chief Stillwater, removing the megaphone, stared blankly.

"Hey?" he bellowed, apparently under the impression that he was still using it.

Larry repeated his question, adding, "And don't yell so about it, either!"

"Dig into?" muttered Stillwater, his mouth ajar. "What do you want to dig into it for?"

Larry's reply was so low I could not hear the words. The fire chief's large mouth gaped still farther.

"My God!" he breathed. "You mean—you think—"

Larry lifted a warning hand.

"Keep it under your hat," he said, almost inaudibly. "Soak it down till it's safe—then let me know. I'll be down at the house. And whatever you do, keep a guard up here and don't let anybody go near it!"

He swung about abruptly.

"Now, Bill," he said, "I want you to help me round up everybody that belongs at Fitch's Folly. Tell them I want to see them in the library right away. You say, Miss Vale's in her room?"

"Yes."

"That leaves"—Larry ticked them off on his fingers—"the butler, the gardener and his wife, Cooper and his wife, old lady Lodge, old Peter and his wife—"

"But she's gone!" I cried, remembering. "Didn't you know it?"

"Who's gone?"

"Nellie Fitch. I took her to the train last night. She had a telegram—"

Larry nodded curtly, his dark face stern in the starlight.

"I'd forgotten," he said, in a tone so odd that I involuntarily stared at him. "Well, I guess that's all—seven of them. And it's going to be the devil's own job locating them. They may be anywhere on the estate—or off it, I suppose, for that matter. Some of them ought to be back at the house by now. Got your flashlight?"

"No. I lost it somewhere."

Larry, turning back to Fire Chief Stillwater, unceremoniously snatched the electric torch from his hand.

"Give me this for awhile, Abel!" he snapped. "I'll see that you get it back!"

"Hey, listen! How'm I going to—"

Larry, ignoring him, thrust the torch at me. "Let's go!" he said.

The next half hour remains a mad phantasmagoria in my memory. To and fro I raced in the darkness, tripping over unseen obstacles, stumbling into unsuspected depressions, directing the beam of my torch into a shifting sea of white faces. Although the crowd had begun to dwindle, it seemed that there must still be hundreds of people milling about the mountain top.

Patty and Gilbert, standing in the front ranks of the spectators surrounding the windmill, were easily found. George Wold I finally located among the sprinkling of watchers remaining at the scene of the forest fire. But of the other four whom I sought I could discover no trace.

And even in this crisis, as I bent every energy to the search, I could not banish from the back of my mind the gnawing and secret fear of the unknown killer which, strive as I would, I could never completely exorcise. What was to prevent him—or her—from striking down victims at will in the darkness and confusion? What assurance had I that I myself, in the next instant, might not be ambushed and murdered?

I was looking nervously over my shoulder as I recrossed the field toward the house. I did not see what lay in my path until I stumbled over something solid and shapeless at its edge.

Picking myself up, I turned my torch downward and stood blinking in amazement at the figure at my feet.

It was that of Karl Litzler, stretched at full length in the grass. His stolid Teutonic countenance was turned toward the sky, and his lips and cheeks were as white as paper.

For a moment I believed I had stumbled upon still another victim of the mysterious murderer who stalked unseen, unknown, across the blackness of the mountain top. But as the light fell full in his eyes he opened them slowly, lifting one feeble hand to shield them from the glare of my torch.

"Who—iss it?" he asked, his voice a mere whisper.

I knelt beside him, placing my hand on his heart. "It's me, Karl— Bill Perley," I reassured him. "What's wrong? What happened?"

Pushing aside my hand, he struggled to a sitting posture.

"My heart—it iss bad," he said, his blue eyes avoiding mine. "The excitement—the running down to the fire, you know. And when I wass coming back—"

"How long have you been here?"

Karl shook his blonde head feebly.

"I know not," he said. "What iss the time?"

Consulting my watch by the light of my torch, I was startled to find it nearly two o'clock. It seemed only moments since the cry of "Fire!" had sent me racing down across the field to the woods.

My thoughts gave a sudden leap.

What woman, alone on the mountain top at midnight, could have discovered the forest fire and given the alarm?

Karl's voice roused me from my musings with a start before I could pursue the subject further.

"The time?" he repeated.

I told him, watching his lowered lids and his swiftly averted gaze. Surely there was something more here than met the eye!

"How long have you been here?" I questioned in turn.

"I know not," he answered evasively. "What hass happened? The master—he iss all right?"

"I hope so, Karl," I said. "Do you feel like walking now? The Chief wants us all up at the house."

With an effort he rose to his feet and stood for a moment breathing deeply, one hand pressed against his heart.

"I try," he said simply.

Guiding him houseward, one hand thrust in his armpit, I strove without success to adjust myself to this new angle of our many-sided problem.

I had believed Karl utterly devoted to the interests of his employer—so much so that I had mentally omitted him from my calculations. I began now to wonder, in the light of his present behavior, if I had been wise.

Had he actually fainted from the effects of excitement and over-exertion on his allegedly weak heart? Or had he too been the victim of a mysterious assault at the hands of someone whom he sought to shield?

Rounding the corner of the house, we came in sight of the crowd about the windmill. Karl stopped short, and I could feel him shivering.

"*Was ist das?*" he cried, reverting momentarily to his native tongue.

I explained briefly, my eyes and thoughts elsewhere. I was wondering whether success had crowned Larry's efforts to round up the occupants of Fitch's Folly, or whether there were still one or more missing.

Karl did not speak when I had finished. I turned to scan his face, lit by a brilliant beam from the window beside us.

To my amaze I found his blue eyes tight shut, his features white and ghastly. He swayed for a moment, leaning so heavily upon my supporting hand that I feared he was about to collapse. Then, recovering himself, he stood staring straight before him, his features a mirror of horror.

"What is it, Karl?" I demanded, shaking him sharply.

He turned toward me a face of dumb helplessness, and for a moment seemed about to speak. Then, shaking his head, he set his lips firmly together.

"Nothing," he said dully. "It iss nothing."

Mystified and more than a little suspicious, I walked silently by his side as he ascended the steps and crossed the porch. The door of the library stood open, and I caught a glimpse of Larry's lanky figure within. There were others, too, but I could not see how many.

At the sound of our footsteps Larry came hurrying out.

"O. K., Bill," he said. "Now will you go upstairs and bring Miss Vale down here?"

Karl, passing him like an automaton, had already entered the room. As I turned away I saw him slump unsteadily into the nearest chair, his eyes still wide with mingled bewilderment and fear.

I ran up the stairs and rapped lightly on Ruth's door.

"It's me—Bill," I said. "Do you feel like coming down to the library now?"

Almost at once the door opened and Ruth appeared, fully clad, on the threshold. She had tinted her cheeks and her lips with rouge and lipstick, but her dark eyes still held the shadow of a hidden horror.

I sketched the status of affairs briefly as we walked together to the head of the staircase. She shivered, glancing uneasily over her shoulder, as we halted momentarily at the spot where I had found her lying unconscious less than an hour earlier.

"When will all this end, Bill?" she asked. "And how?"

"I wish I knew," I answered as soberly.

Descending the stairs, I followed her into the library. Larry was already speaking, his voice harsh and resonant, his grim features weary but still determined.

"I believed that I had taken all possible precautions against a third death," he was saying as I entered. "But I'm afraid it has happened, in spite of everything. A search of the shack will tell—and that will be made as soon as it cools sufficiently and as soon as I have finished here.

"In the meantime, of course, it is possible that he may still be somewhere in the grounds. Or, for that matter, he may have been kidnapped--"

Puzzled, I stared about me, counting silently to myself. Who was missing? Patty and Gilbert, Ruth, Margery and George, Karl, Alice Lodge—surely that made seven!

Then, with a thrill of horror, I remembered that Larry's original count had excluded Ruth. And in the same instant I realized the identity of the sole absentee.

Peter Fitch, whose fear of death by fire had been his constant obsession, had not been found!

CHAPTER XV
A REAL CLUE

You who have followed this chronicle thus far may feel, perhaps justifiably, that you are not being treated fairly in the matter of clues. In these pages you will fail to find the detailed diagram, the cigarette butt, the mudstain, the fingerprint, the telltale time schedule, the trickily phrased interrogation with its revelatory replies, and all the other customary paraphernalia of detection.

For these omissions, my apologies. They cannot be helped. I am merely telling the tale of those July days as their dread panorama unrolled itself before my own eyes from ominous morning to fear-filled night.

Some intimate member of the household, doubtless, could have told this story more satisfactorily and with fewer gaps. For I was, after all, an outsider, save in such measure as Larry had enlisted my aid. And although a chauffeur, rating as a mere stage prop, may often absorb surprising information, I felt myself lucky—or unlucky—to have been able to see and hear as much as I did.

With this apology, therefore, I return to Larry's grilling of the group in the library, which unfortunately proved a flat failure. The whole picture had been so muddled by the midnight forest blaze that no one seemed able to say with any certainty where they or anyone else had been at any particular moment. It proved practically impossible, moreover, in view of the circumstances, to verify what few coherent statements were obtainable.

It was past three o'clock in the morning before Larry, his face dark with passion, crashed his fist down on the table and rose abruptly to his feet.

"So help me God," he said, his harsh voice shaking, "sometimes I think every last one of you is involved in this! How you can sit there protesting your innocence and let this hellish business go on night after night, is more than I can understand! And I'll take oath that some of the rest of you are holding back something—something that might help if we only knew about it!"

I glanced involuntarily at Ruth, to find her gaze fixed questioningly upon me. Fearing she was about to speak, I shook my head ever so little. This was decidedly not the time and place for her to reveal her knowledge.

In the dead silence that followed, my gaze leaped swiftly from face to face. I could not but admire—if one may call it that—the utter sang froid displayed by every member of the group under Larry's browbeating.

Was the criminal possessed of iron nerves and a constitution of chilled steel? Or was Larry, after all, on the wrong track entirely?

My eyes turned back to the Vershire chief. He still stood motionless behind the table, his eyes glinting like chips of jade. The silence lengthened interminably before he spoke.

"It's nearly daylight," he said curtly. "You might as well retire for now. But if any of you try to make a break before this case is cleared up, I'll follow him to the ends of the earth and bring him back and send him to the chair for murder!"

And on this melodramatic note the huddled group, silent and white-faced, dissolved. Larry, standing just inside the open door, did not turn until the last faint footstep had died away and the last door had clicked shut.

"Well, I hope I scared somebody," he said with a wry, one-sided smile. "If they'd stop to think, they'd know I can't prove a thing—yet. But I can't afford to spend time chasing anybody that gets cold feet—"

"How about Nellie Fitch?" I could not help asking.

"Oh, I know all about that," said Larry. "She'll be back sometime tomorrow—today, I mean."

"What makes you so sure?" I asked.

Larry eyed me oddly.

"Well, she'll hear her husband has disappeared, won't she?" he argued.

"What do you mean, 'disappeared'?"

"I couldn't tell you, Bill. At least he isn't here. But whether he's been murdered, or kidnapped, or just plain run away—"

He turned abruptly toward the door.

"Let's see how things stand up at the windmill," he said.

The first faint streaks of morning gleamed behind the eastward ranges as we emerged into the open air. I felt an acute pang of nausea, compounded of weariness, sleeplessness, and sheer unadulterated nerves, as I moved mechanically in Larry's footsteps through the unreal gray of the summer dawn. I have never since seen a sunrise without feeling the ghastly hand of memory plucking at the pit of my stomach.

The fire apparatus had departed; the group about the ruins had dwindled to a scant score. In the forefront of the scattered spectators I noted, with a grim inward chuckle, the twin bulks of Williams and Peabody—firmly anchored, apparently, by the scathing sarcasm of their chief.

The charred and water-soaked heap beneath the soot-smeared steel uprights showed no sign of smoke beneath the rays of Larry's torch. The beam flickered over the half-burned timbers as he made a complete circuit of the windmill. Then, turning to Stillwater, he jerked his thumb toward the debris.

"Start your men digging there," he directed. "Tell them to take it easy. I'll hold the torch till it gets light. It won't be long now."

But it was not until the sun, creeping slowly upward into view, was bathing the mountain top in the fresh beauty of a new day, that the ghastly secret of the windmill shack lay revealed in all its hideousness.

The bones of the skeleton, half consumed by the fierce heat, were those of a man of less than medium stature. They lay face downward, exposing the round, bony convexity at the top and rear of the skull. The features—if you could call them that—were half buried in the ashes. It was a gruesome sight, and for once even the loud-mouthed fire chief was silent.

Larry, his face expressionless, stood staring down at the skeleton for a long moment, his shoulders sagging wearily. His face, in the pitiless light of morning, was that of a man nearing the end of both physical and nervous resources.

"Well, we've got it all to do over again," he said tonelessly. "Call up Doc Reefer and Gene Hawkins, Bill. Tell them to get up here as soon as they can."

Skirting the silent house, I climbed the stairs to my room. Here, by means of the intercommunicating phone system, I got through to the Vershire exchange and shortly had routed both the county solicitor and the medical referee from their beds.

Utterly spent, I propped myself in my window to await their arrival. I must have dozed, for the sound of Hawkins' car brought me to with a start.

I hurried down the stairs and along the ridge in the wake of the official pair, drawn both by morbid curiosity and by a dogged desire to see things through. Doc Reefer was just turning the skeleton over when I arrived.

Although the flesh had been partially burned from the bones, the front of the skull seemed to have escaped the full heat of the flames. It lay staring up at us from its hollow eyeholes with a hideous fixed gaze that made my skin creep.

"Well?" demanded Larry harshly, his voice loud in the silence. "Is it Peter Fitch, or isn't it?"

Doc Reefer, still kneeling, looked up over his shoulder. Once again I was incongruously reminded of a huge sparrow with its head on one side.

"Hard to say, Larry," he answered. "Unless—"

"Unless what?" snapped Larry as he paused.

"Did the old—did he have false teeth?"

"Yes!" said Larry and I in unison.

Doc Reefer, bending above the skull, pried open its tightly clenched jaws with his muscular hands, an act which caused a fresh pang in the pit of my stomach. A moment later he turned toward us.

"Well—here they are!" he said.

I stared into his cupped hands in horrified fascination. Although the hard rubber holding the porcelain had been partially melted by the fierce heat, the teeth themselves, grotesquely out of line, still grinned hideously at us with the semblance of a sardonic smile.

"How do you know they're Peter Fitch's?" demanded Larry.

The medical referee shrugged his broad shoulders.

"I don't," he said. "That's a job for the dentist—always supposing he had them made here. If he didn't—well, it's going to be harder, that's all."

Larry nodded assent.

"I'll say it is," he admitted. "Check them downtown for me if you can—will you, Doc? And be sure there's no mistake about it. I don't see as there's much else to go on."

Doc Reefer, thrusting the dentures in his pocket, shook his huge head doubtfully.

"There isn't," he said. "Clothes all burned off, of course—unless you can find some buttons or something. I'll try to make some sort of an autopsy, but I doubt if it will help. Looks like a possible fracture at the base of the skull. Might have been caused by a beam falling on it, though. Want me to wait for the undertaker? He'll be here any minute now—I notified him before I left."

"Might as well," nodded Larry, and fell to raking over the ashes about the skeleton. In a few moments he had a handful of buttons—which later, I may as well state here, were positively identified by Nellie Fitch as belonging to the suit her husband had worn constantly since his arrival that summer at Fitch's Folly.

I have only a confused impression of the next couple of hours—the departure of Doc Reefer and the undertaker, trailed by Solicitor Hawkins; the stationing of Williams and Peabody, near dead for sleep, outside the still silent house with the strictest sort of orders from their chief; the agonizing cat-naps caught by Larry and myself in the backbreaking library chairs.

We both came wide awake, however, at the first shrill trill of the phone. Doc Reefer's full tones, pouring from the receiver, were clearly audible to me on the opposite side of the table.

"You're in luck, Larry," he said. "Doc O'Neill made those very plates for old man Fitch four years ago—said the ones he had made in New York got loose or something."

"He identifies them, then?"

"Absolutely. He put a gold band on one of the eye teeth for camouflage. Fitch insisted on having it—thought 'twould make 'em look more like natural teeth. As if anybody wouldn't know the old goat was wearing false ones!"

Recalling old Peter's objectionable habit, I could not but mentally concur. Certainly no one who went about clacking his dentures together, as he did, could be said to create a wholly successful illusion.

"So it is old Peter, after all," said Larry thoughtfully.

"Don't see who else it could be," came Doc's booming reply. "Nobody else missing, is there?"

"No," admitted Larry with perplexing reluctance.

"O. K., then. Now I'll get at the autopsy. If anything new shows up, I'll give you a buzz. 'Bye."

Larry, hanging up, sat staring dully across the table at me. Dark shadows showed beneath his dark eyes, and his face, pasty and colorless, was lined with utter fatigue.

"Swell!" he muttered. "Now we've got two skeletons with circumstantial identification! If we get another one, I'll go nuts!"

"But this one is absolute!" I expostulated. "And Guy's—"

"Guy's? Horsefeathers! The skeleton's teeth were perfect, and so were Guy's. Therefore, the skeleton was Guy's. If that's logic, I'm a moron!"

"That's different," I was forced to admit. "But this time—surely O'Neill couldn't be mistaken!"

"I suppose not," muttered Larry. "But all the same, anything could have happened up here after the forest fire was set to draw us away from the house—"

"You think the fire was set?"

"I'm practically positive of it, Bill. After all, coincidence can stretch only so far."

His broad shoulders sagged as he lifted the receiver and gave the number of the police station.

"Might as well get this over with," he said from the corner of his mouth. "I'm not— Hello— Jim? Larry speaking. Heard the latest? Yes, it's the old man this time. Yes, he's been identified. Body found in the windmill shack. Doc Reefer's making an autopsy. Jesse and Zenas will give you the dope— I'm sending them down to get some sleep. No, there's no clue—as usual!

"You'd better break the news to the reporters and tell them to keep right on keeping away from here! They won't get any more if they come up—and if I catch one trying to sneak in, I'll throw him clear off the top of the mountain!"

It occurs to me at this point that I have heretofore omitted mention of the press, to which affairs at Fitch's Folly were rapidly assuming national importance. The chain of events inaugurated with Guy's death and continuing through the attack on old Peter and the murder of Martha had set the metropolitan journalists agog. I shuddered to think of the sensation which news of the death of the Albany millionaire would create.

Fitch's Folly itself, however, had so far been kept free from the journalistic pests styled special writers, who congregate about a mystery or a murder like buzzards about carrion. By joint agreement of the Fitch family, which abhorred publicity, and Larry Frost, who shared their views, a strict ban had been placed on the premises; and though bodily ejection of several ambitious news photographers had been necessary, the cluster of news men congregated at Vershire had for the most part taken the ban philosophically.

But now, with Peter Fitch's murder splashed across the headlines, there would be no holding them. The head of the Fitch clan, despite the comparative seclusion in which he had lived of late, had always been front page news; his death, climaxing the series of holocausts at Fitch's Folly, would unquestionably be the signal for a fresh influx of keyhole peepers of the most virulent type.

Abandoning these gloomy musings, I looked up to find Larry eyeing me speculatively.

"Bill," he said, "I know you're dead for sleep. But do you suppose you could carry on here for awhile?"

"Sure," I said, stifling a yawn. "What are you going to do?"

"I've got to meet Vickery and those two birds he's bringing back from Hartford. It's obvious now, of course, that neither of them could have been involved in the old man's death. But all the same, I'm going to have them bound over—always supposing that Gene agrees. And if I get a chance, Bill, I've simply got to get some sleep myself. This business is beginning to get under my skin."

Eyeing him narrowly, I was forced to admit the truth of his statement. The four hectic days and nights through which he had passed had taken heavy toll of Larry Frost. He looked like a man on the edge of a nervous breakdown.

"I'd forgotten all about those two," I said. "Where do you figure they fit in—or don't you?"

"I don't know, Bill. Yesterday I had a theory. But today—"

"What was it?" I interrupted eagerly.

Larry shook his head.

"It didn't prove up," he said, and would say no more.

Shortly thereafter he departed, leaving in his wake a fresh detachment of firemen sifting the ashes of the windmill shack for additional clues. He also, to my mystification, had Forbes broadcast a description of Peter Fitch, which seemed to me the height of inconsistency.

"Queer thing, the way that body'd been burned," he said just before leaving. "A fire no bigger than that wouldn't have consumed the flesh completely; it must have been soaked in kerosene. And say, Bill—I wish you'd locate all the kerosene on the place and dump it or get rid of it. I should have done it before, of course. When I think of all the things I should have done and didn't—"

Stamping viciously on the starter, he roared away down the winding road.

I stood staring after him until he had vanished beyond the iron gates. The torrid west wind had died with the dawn, but the still air on the mountain top was unbelievably hot.

Although the morning was now well advanced, the big house seemed still sunk in slumber, its windows curtained and blank. I did catch a glimpse of the face of Alice Lodge, framed in curl papers, staring down at me from the window of one of the unoccupied rooms; but as I looked, it vanished, and did not reappear.

I made my way to the kitchen, where Margery, her black hair hanging dankly about her face, was fuming over the failure of the family to appear for breakfast. She found no cause for complaint in my appetite, for I was undisguisedly ravenous.

I watched her narrowly as I stowed away the ample repast—always, I am frank to admit, when her piercing black eyes were not fixed upon me. I found myself recalling, with a feeling strongly resembling fear, the waxen image I had found in her room that morning.

Rising to leave, I drew a bow at a venture.

"Where's Wenty?" I asked without warning.

Margery's sultry eyes suddenly shot twin shafts of black fire.

"I don't know!" she flared. "And if I did, I wouldn't tell you—any of you! Persecuting a poor innocent boy for something he didn't do—"

I fled hastily, pursued by the crescendo of her voice. I could still hear it after I had slammed shut the kitchen door.

Recalling Larry's orders, I proceeded to check up on the kerosene. The only can I could find, however, was the five-gallon container on the rear porch which held the supply used for summer cooking in the oil stove. This, however, proved to be empty, and the one-gallon can with the snouted top, used to transfer the fuel to the stove, was missing.

Ending my futile search, I wandered aimlessly about the grounds and through the still unbelievably quiet house, coming at last to rest in the library. En route I had collected the New York *Herald-Tribune*, tossed on the porch by Ted Nicholls, the milkman, on his morning visit to Fitch's Folly.

Until then, so hectic had been the events of the early morning hours, I had not realized that it was Sunday.

I recalled clearly old Peter, steel-rimmed spectacles astride his prominent nose, scanning the columns of his favorite Sunday sheet with his opaque, slaty eyes. Despite the fact that I had cherished no particular love for my late employer, I found my red-rimmed eyes burning queerly at realization that he at last had been overtaken by the fate he so long had feared.

Spreading the voluminous pages atop the table, I riffled them idly, with some vague idea of finding a job through the classified columns. The next instant the rotogravure section opened under my aimless fingers, and a picture in the center of the left hand page hit me squarely between the eyes.

It was an Atlantic City scene showing a merry party, scantily clad, grouped about a central pair on the Boardwalk. It was obvious, from the prominence given the picture, that its subjects were members of Gotham's so-called Four Hundred, and the caption—"Mr. and Mrs. Z. Terwilliger Jones and Party of Long Island Enjoying the Salt Sea Breezes"—was all but superfluous.

But it was not the Joneses themselves who had caught my attention. It was rather the figure of a man standing apart, his thick dark hair brushed smoothly back from his forehead, his gaunt frame encased in an ill-fitting bathing suit, his mien obviously one of non-merriment.

It was none of these features, however, which gripped my gaze. It was the deep-set, piercing eyes, staring straight into the camera.

I recalled all too plainly where I had seen such a pair of eyes.

Unless he possessed a perfect twin whose scalp was as hairy as his own was hairless, the man enjoying the salt sea breezes on the Boardwalk with Mr. and Mrs. Z. Terwilliger Jones was none other than the missing Dinwiddie!

CHAPTER XVI
GRIM WARNING

I sat staring incredulously at the pictured I countenance before me. The baffling feature was the inexplicable growth of hair as contrasted with Dinwiddie's polished baldness. But when I covered the upper third of the picture with my thumb, the likeness was unmistakable.

My knowledge of the rotogravure process told me that the picture had been taken some time before the current issue of the paper—certainly before Dinwiddie's visit to Fitch's Folly. I scanned the finer print beneath, but it yielded no clue. I felt certain, however, that the unknown could be identified, though probably not without some difficulty.

I reached for the phone to pass the word on to Larry, but before I could lift the receiver the bell rang sharply.

"Hello?" I said.

"That you, Perley?"

I almost dropped the receiver in astonishment. For the voice was indubitably that of Nellie Fitch, whom only the previous evening I had seen safely aboard the train for New York!

"Yes, Madam," I said, striving to conceal my surprise.

"Bring the car down to the station immediately! If I have to wait here much longer in this heat, I'll be fried like an egg!"

"Yes, Madam," I said promptly. "I'll be down at once."

Still pondering the puzzle of her rapid-fire return and the accuracy of Larry's prediction, I backed the limousine out of the garage and headed for Vershire. A swift survey of the scene as I departed showed all apparently serene and peaceful; even yet, save for Alice Lodge, no one seemed to be astir.

I arrived to find Nellie Fitch, her horse-like face red and moist, striding up and down the platform. She began her tirade even before I could get out of the car.

"—senseless wild goose chase!" were the first words that assailed my astonished ears. "If I could find out who was responsible for a trick like that, I'd make it mighty hot for them! And Grace playing contract as lively as you please when I came dashing up to the apartment in a taxi at two o'clock in the morning—"

"You mean—she was all right?" I broke in, blinking.

"All right?" screeched Nellie Fitch, her crimson cheeks puffing out like twin balloons. "It was a deliberate deception! Vinson never sent any such wire—and Grace hadn't been in a car all day! I felt like a fool, bursting in on them like that! I took a cab straight back to the station and caught the first train out—I wanted to find out what sort of skullduggery's afoot here!"

She paused, but only for breath.

"And before you take me home," she resumed with unabated vigor, "you'll take me to the telegraph office! I'm going to find out—"

She stopped short, eyeing me shrewdly. It had just occurred to me that she must be in utter ignorance of old Peter's death, and I have never boasted the possession of a poker face.

"What's wrong, Perley?" she demanded in an altered tone.

"Have you heard from—from home since you left?" I asked awkwardly enough.

"No. What's happened?"

"It's—your husband, Madam. He's—"

I hesitated, unwilling to pronounce thus baldly old Peter's fate. But Nellie Fitch, though the color drained from her raddled cheeks, completed the sentence with characteristic brusqueness.

"Dead, is he?" she barked. "Well, tell me about it! Don't stand there with your mouth open!"

I caught her arm as she swayed slightly.

"It's the heat," she snapped, recovering herself, and climbed a little unsteadily into the rear seat. "There, that's better—that sun was terrible! Now tell me all about it, Perley."

As gently as I could, I outlined the dread events of the night just past. She took it sitting bolt upright, but the lines of her weather-worn face deepened as she listened.

She sat silent, mopping her brick-red face with her handkerchief, when I had finished, Then, after an ominous pause:

"Take me to the county solicitor!" she snapped.

"He wasn't there at all last night, Madam," I said uneasily. "Chief Frost—"

"Never mind Chief Frost! He's bungled this case all he's going to! Take me to Hawkins!"

Aghast at this sudden turn of affairs, I set my lips together and followed orders.

Nellie Fitch, alighting in front of the block which housed Gene Hawkins' office, stood regarding me bleakly.

"Call for me in fifteen minutes!" she commanded at length, and marched into the building with an air which boded no good to Larry.

I drove at once to the police station. Larry, however, was in the courtroom with his prisoners. He would, Jim Forbes assured me, be at liberty in a moment.

Taking advantage of the opportunity, I slipped down the street to the Western Union office. But here the operator, whom I knew but slightly, told a straightforward and convincing story.

The wire, he said, had arrived through regular channels the previous afternoon, with nothing to indicate any irregularity. In accordance with previous instructions from Fitch's Folly forbidding the phoning of telegrams, he assured me earnestly, he had left his assistant in charge, had taken it directly to the estate in person in his own car, and had delivered it into the hands of Nellie Fitch herself.

Vaguely disappointed, I hurried back to Larry's office.

The Vershire police chief, his long legs cocked on the corner of his desk, his No. 12s perched heel to toe in an imposing monument, regarded me unblinkingly as I blurted out the nature of Nellie Fitch's present errand.

"Fine!" he said. "Now I can get some sleep!"

"What?" I gasped unbelievingly.

"Sure!" said Larry grimly. "Let Gene and Oscar take a crack at it for a change—let's see how far they get!"

I stared at him in astonishment.

"Larry!" I burst out. "You don't mean—you're going to throw in your hand without a scrap? Why, those two will never find out anything in a thousand years!"

"What do I care?" snapped Larry. "Right now I could sleep that long and still be only half caught up! What's that paper sticking out of your pocket?"

I had completely forgotten the rotogravure section I had brought down from Fitch's Folly. Now, unfolding it, I pointed to the picture.

"Who's that?" demanded Larry, pouncing upon it.

Hesitantly I voiced my belief. Larry, his weary eyes gleaming anew, squinted at the studio copyright below.

"Underwood & Underwood," he said. "Ought to be able to trace that, seems as though. However, if what you say is true, that'll be Gene's job, not mine."

He slumped back into his chair, eyeing me stonily. I struggled for words to voice my bewilderment, but none came.

"You might be interested to know," he said after a moment, "that perhaps my last official act in this case was to persuade Gene to have those two birds from Hartford bound over and sent to the county jail. We didn't have a thing on them, as a matter of fact, but I talked him into holding them until we got this mess straightened out. Now, I'll bet you money, the first thing he'll do will be to turn them loose again!"

Swiveling about, he stared blankly out of the window, his broad shoulders sagging.

"Larry," I finally got out with difficulty, "we've—I've been helping you—or trying to. What'll I do now?"

Larry, his voice flat and expressionless, spoke without turning his head.

"Right now," he said, "you'd better go and collect old lady Fitch. She just went past the end of the alley, looking as mad as hops. If she catches you chumming around with me right now, she'll probably fire you too!"

Piqued, I made my departure without another word. It was easy to understand Larry's bitterness at his impending removal from the case, after the work he had done and the sleepless nights he had spent. But, knowing him as I thought I did, I could not imagine him quitting cold without a struggle.

I avoided embarrassing questions by circling the block before appearing on Main Street to pick up Nellie Fitch. My spirits soared somewhat as I drove her homeward in silence. Perhaps, after all, she had changed her mind; perhaps Hawkins had refused to depose Larry. I hoped fervently that such was the case.

My hopes were dashed, however, directly after lunch, when I saw the old-fashioned, high-posted sedan of the county solicitor come chugging up the driveway. Beside him, I noted as it drew nearer, set Sheriff Oscar Vickery.

Heretofore I have mentioned Sheriff Vickery but briefly; he deserves, even at this point, only a thumbnail sketch. He was a tall, corpse-like individual with a glass eye and large, hairy hands; and he had never, under any circumstances, been known to remove his hat. It was probably untrue, however, that he slept in it. His criminological ability was about on a par with that of Solicitor Hawkins, who now clambered out of the dust-covered sedan and mounted the steps with an air of mingled self-importance and trepidation.

What progress the pair made with their so-called investigation during the ensuing hours I did not know and did not greatly care. I was satisfied that they could learn little that Larry did not already know. An occasional glance through the library window revealed some progressive inquisition going forward, but I lacked sufficient interest even to eavesdrop.

I had washed the limousine and was polishing it when I saw them depart, looking rather less self-important and considerably more worried. It was perhaps an hour later that I heard my phone ring and mounted the stairs two at a time to answer it. "Bring the limousine around at once, Perley," I was ordered.

Halting it beneath the porte-cochère, I found a general exodus in order. Nellie Fitch led the parade into the car, followed by Alice Lodge, Patty and Gilbert, and even Ruth.

"Judge Manning's office!" she commanded.

Two deputies stood guard at the iron gates, one of them arguing vehemently with a news cameraman. At sight of us the photographer, skipping nimbly to the side of the road, leveled his apparatus at the oncoming car.

I twitched the wheel, sending the heavy limousine directly at him. Paling, he leaped backward, tripped, and fell sprawling. I could well imagine what the car had looked like in the view finder.

There were more cameramen and more news men in front of Judge Manning's office. Hawkins and Vickery, waiting on the sidewalk, were fairly surrounded, and neither seemed averse to the attention bestowed upon them.

"Wait here, Perley!" ordered Nellie Fitch.

"Yes, Madam," I said, touching my cap.

"And don't talk!"

"Certainly not, Madam."

Cameras clicked as she stalked stiffly across the sidewalk, disdaining even to draw her veil. Mrs. Lodge followed timidly, her mouse-gray eyes shuttering from side to side. Gilbert, his arm about his bride, sought vainly to shield her from the barrage. Ruth, last to leave the car, spared me a whimsical, troubled glance before braving the battery of gleaming lenses.

Solicitor Hawkins, ushering them within, turned to wave back the importunate throng.

"I can't say another word now, boys," he announced importantly, tugging at his scrap of side whisker. "Perhaps after the will is read I'll be able to give you something more. No, I don't know the terms. The Judge tells me it is a new will, executed three days ago. Now if you'll excuse me—"

He vanished into the hallway, where, before the door closed, I caught a glimpse of the corpse-like form of Sheriff Vickery.

I sat stonily erect in the driver's seat, ignoring both queries and cameras, until the pack of interrogators beat a retreat accelerated by a sudden sharp shower which drove them to cover. Beneath my indifference, however, I was seething with curiosity.

Three days ago!

That had been the day, I now recalled, that I had taken old Peter to see Judge Manning, ostensibly about Wenty's incarceration. Of a certainty their conference had occupied an extended period of time, but at the moment I had thought nothing of it. It was easy now to fathom the source of the old man's elation on his return trip.

I could not help wondering exactly what had motivated the new will. The obvious reason, naturally, was the death of his son Guy. But I felt certain, without definite basis for the belief, that some other factor was also involved.

Was it in some way connected with the series of crimes? Would its reading, perhaps, provide some new and startling revelation?

A half hour later I realized that my belief, after all, had not been baseless. I studied the faces of my passengers as they emerged in silence, noting the subtle alteration which had taken place. It was evident that some sort of a bombshell had been exploded in the Judge's office.

They were ushered to the car by Solicitor Hawkins, whose earlier air of importance had grown appreciably. He waved back the reporters as they clustered eagerly about him.

"Sorry, boys," he said with specious geniality. "Can't give you a thing right now. The sheriff and I have some things to see to first. But the minute anything breaks—"

"What's going to break?" demanded a sharp-nosed scribe. "An arrest?"

Hawkins assumed an air of mystery.

"Well, I wouldn't go as far as to say that right now," he replied. "But we believe we've got hold of something—"

Reluctantly I set the car in motion as a peremptory rap sounded on the glass panel behind my head. I had heard just enough to rouse my curiosity without satisfying it.

Were Hawkins and Vickery following up a false clue? Or had old Peter's will contained information of real value?

I wondered, as I drove slowly down Main Street, what Larry Frost was doing. Had I realized that the conference in the Judge's office would take so long, I would have risked a flying visit to police headquarters.

Before I had turned in at the entrance to the mountain road, I became aware that the car I was piloting might well have been filled with mourners en route to a funeral. My five passengers, glimpsed in the windshield mirror, sat staring straight ahead, their faces thoughtful and preoccupied. And save for a few mumbled and meaningless words, but one voice reached my ears on the homeward trip.

It was that of Alice Lodge, rising shrill with sudden hysteria.

"I can't believe it!" she cried. "Why should Peter—"

"*Ssssh!* What if he should hear you? He might—"

The rest was a whisper, indistinguishable to my straining ears. But the little that I had heard gave me, as the saying is, furiously to think.

Perspiration, due not wholly to the heat, exuded from my pores as I drove up the winding road. Of a sudden I found myself missing Larry intensely.

It was with scant success that I sought to persuade myself that the volume of death had been closed once and for all with the third and last of the series—the murder of Peter Fitch, who from the first had voiced his fear of a violent end. Surely, I told myself, the carnival of crime had ceased, and we all might sleep soundly once more in our beds that night.

Inwardly, however, I remained utterly unconvinced. Somehow I felt certain, even then, that we had not reached the end; that the un-seen slayer, torch in hand, still crouched hidden, skulking, ready to spring.

The sight of Fitch's Folly, as we emerged from the forest and passed through the gate into the spacious grounds, failed to dispel this premonition. There was something sinister about its bulk, life-less and monstrous, looming huge against the western sky.

For all that we had left at least five persons on the premises, the house seemed absolutely deserted; of living soul, as far as I could see, there was no sign anywhere.

Beneath its sheen of perspiration I felt my scalp prickle eerily. My nerves crawled as I drove slowly along the gravel and came to a halt beneath the porte-cochère. Surely something was sadly amiss!

I was totally unprepared, however, for the actual eventuality. As I stopped, the front door burst open and Karl, racing across the porch, fairly leaped down the steps. His Teutonic features were livid, and his hands, as he scrabbled frantically at the door of the limousine, were shaking like those of a man utterly unstrung.

Reaching across, I grabbed him by the arm. He turned toward me, his blue eyes wide and staring.

"The killer!" he gasped. "The murderer! He iss—still here!"

"Here? Where? What do you mean?"

For answer he held out a crumpled sheet of paper on which I saw words crudely printed.

"I found this—in the hall!" he stammered. "just now—I wass com-ing down—"

I snatched the sheet from his hand. Its warning, sprawling crazily across the page, fulfilled my worst fears.

IF THE REST OF YOU DON'T WANT TO GET WHAT
PETER FITCH GOT—DON'T STAY HERE TONIGHT!

CHAPTER XVII
MYSTERY MESSAGE

"What is it, Perley?"

Nellie Fitch's strident voice recalled me at least partially to sanity. I held the paper toward the open window of the limousine.

"Karl found this in the hall," I said, none too steadily. "He said he—"

The note was yanked abruptly from my grasp. A rising murmur of incredulity and horror followed as it passed from hand to hand inside the car.

I turned back to the trembling butler, who seemed on the verge of collapse.

"What do you know about this, Karl?" I demanded sternly.

"*Mein Gott*, Bill—I know nothing! Just now I wass coming along the hall—"

"What hall?"

"The upstairs hall. I see this paper at the top of the stairs, and I pick it up, and I read it. And yoost then I hear the car coming—"

"And you ran out with the note?"

"Ach, yess! I wass scared—"

I seized him firmly by the arm.

"Listen, Karl!" I said.

"Yess?"

"Have you seen any suspicious-looking persons hanging around here since we left?"

Karl shook his head violently.

"No, Bill. I haf been here all afternoon—"

"Right here in the house?"

"Yess."

"Could anyone have come in here without your knowing it?"

"No—I swear it!"

Leaving Karl gaping, I hurried past him into the house. But a rapid-fire interrogation of its occupants—Margery, Della, and Mary—served only to corroborate Karl's statement.

All had been busy in various parts of the house during our absence; all swore that no one could have entered without their knowledge. Either one or more of them was lying, or the secret of Fitch's Folly had not even approached its ultimate solution.

The three domestics, still protesting their innocence, followed me out onto the porch. I looked about for George, but the gardener was apparently occupied elsewhere.

"Perley!"

"Yes, Madam?"

"We've made up our minds," said Nellie Fitch. "We're staying at the Vershire Inn tonight. This may all be some fool's idea of a joke—but if it is, we're willing to be the goat! And if that Hawkins doesn't get to the bottom of it in a hurry—"

She paused, glaring belligerently at the group on the porch.

"You three are at liberty to leave if you wish," she said. "I'm sure I wouldn't ask anyone to stay—"

"We were just going home anyway, ma'am," piped Della and Mary in chorus.

"How about you, Margery? I'll get you and George a room at the Inn, too."

Margery's black eyes were smoldering fires.

"It's very nice of you, I'm sure, Mrs. Fitch," she answered sullenly. "But I've never yet been afraid of man nor devil—and I don't intend to begin now!"

"You mean—you'll stay?" squalled Nellie Fitch.

Margery's eyes were inscrutable.

"I'll stay," she said slowly.

"And George?"

"He'll stay, too!" said Margery grimly, adding under her breath, "And like it!"

Nellie Fitch turned to Karl with a snort. "You'll go?" she asked.

Karl's face grew slowly ashen. The whites of his pale blue eyes showed as their pupils shuttered hideously from side to side.

"No, Madam," he said painfully. "I stay."

"Well, Perley? I'm sure you'd love to stay, too?"

My hesitation was only momentary. I was afraid—deadly afraid—of what might happen that night on the mountain top. But the refusal of both Margery and Karl to leave in the face of obvious danger had roused my curiosity. I knew that Larry would never have ignored so promising a lead.

"If you don't mind, Madam," I answered.

Nellie Fitch snorted again—a wheezing, horsey snort that accentuated the equine lines of her face.

"Well, I'm sure I don't care what all you fools do," she said tersely. "Remember, I disclaim all responsibility. That warning is enough for us. Perley, you stay here while we pack some things."

The exodus of the dwellers at Fitch's Folly, which took place in record time, had all the earmarks of a general rout. One by one they came hurrying through the doorway, casting apprehensive glances behind them. Alice Lodge, last to leave, was fairly running.

"What's the matter with you?" snapped her half-sister.

"I—I don't know! I thought I heard something—"

"Stuff and nonsense! Get in here and stop shivering so! All right, Perley!"

The shadows of late afternoon were lengthening across the valley as I drove the fugitives down the winding road. There was something cozy and cheering in the sight of the town of Vershire nestling among the foothills below me. I began to regret my rash resolve to spend the night at Fitch's Folly—with my sole companions a Teuton, a dullard, and a madwoman!

It was still light, however, upon the mountain top when I returned. As I drove into the garage I caught a fleeting glimpse, along the westward path, of Della and Mary, scuttling like scared hens for their homes beyond the wall before dusk should descend.

My first act was a renewed scrutiny of the interior of the huge house, with particular emphasis on the second floor, where the mystery message had made its appearance. But I found nothing more incriminating than an irregular spot of moisture on one of the

ceilings, where the brief afternoon downpour had evidently penetrated the ancient shingles of the roof above.

My footsteps echoed hollowly down the empty corridors and
through the deserted rooms. I was glad enough to leave the upper
regions and descend to the more cozy kitchen, where I came upon
Karl snatching a hasty meal.

I regarded him curiously as I seated myself. Since that morning
he had figured almost constantly in my thoughts as the murderer.
But now, eyeing his pale face, his troubled blue eyes, his stiff, straw-
colored hair, I could not find it in my heart to believe him guilty of
the triple crime.

"Why are you staying here tonight, Karl?" I asked abruptly.

He gave a violent start, and his eyes refused to meet mine.

"It iss my duty to keep watch on the house," he replied. "I haf
been told not to leave—"

"Who told you?"

Karl, shaking his head, began to wolf down the contents of his
plate in an obvious effort to shorten the interview.

"But aren't you afraid?" I persisted maliciously.

Karl's hands began to shake violently, although for a moment he
kept his eyes fixed upon his plate. Then he lifted his head, and the
words came in a flood.

"Afraid?" he repeated, his lips livid. "Who would not be afraid?
I understand nothing—nothing! The master's enemies—why should
they kill first his son and then his son's *Frau*? Willingly would I leave
tonight—but I dare not! I haf my orders! This note—iss it a joke? I
know not! I am confused! What should I do? Once before I haf followed orders—and while I did—"

He gulped and fell silent, his pale eyes flickering furtively.

"And while you did?" I prompted with unconcealed eagerness.

"It iss nothing," he mumbled, and would say no more.

"So you think the note may be a joke?" I inquired.

Karl shook his head hopelessly.

"I know not," he repeated. "But no one could haf come in here
this afternoon—I swear it, Bill! If it iss not black magic—"

He broke off, staring past me. I swiveled about, to see Margery
Wold standing in the doorway.

Clearing his plate with a final sweep of his fork, Karl rose stumblingly and left the room, his face as white as chalk. Margery vanished also, but not before her sudden appearance had diverted my thoughts into a new channel.

What if Margery herself had placed the warning note at the head of the staircase? What if, possessed of secret knowledge of Wenty's presence on the mountain top, she had taken this method to terrify the Fitches and drive them from the Folly while she hid him more securely, or even arranged for his escape?

My musings were interrupted by the sound of a car hammering up the driveway. Hurrying through the house, I reached the porch in time to meet Solicitor Hawkins and Sheriff Vickery tiptoeing up the steps.

The former, fairly bursting with importance, beckoned me forward. His stage whisper could have been heard fifty feet away.

"Where's Litzler?" he hissed.

"Who?"

"That Litzler fellow—the butler! Quick!"

"W-why—he was right here a few minutes ago!" I stuttered, startled. "What—"

Sheriff Vickery's fishy eye gleamed as he lunged past me. I swung about to see him gripping Karl's shoulder with one hairy hand and thrusting a gun into the butler's midriff with the other.

"Karl Litzler," he intoned, for all the world like an old-time stock company villain, "I arrest you for the murder of Peter Fitch!"

I stood staring stupefied, unable to believe my ears. Was this quiet, loyal, timid figure, with his blue eyes and straw-colored hair, the lunatic killer who had struck down his employer, soaked his corpse in kerosene, and made of the windmill shack a flaming torch and a funeral pyre?

Karl, his features pasty, looked equally dazed. His pale eyes blinked entreatingly.

"I did not—do it!" he said numbly, his lips quivering.

"'S what they all say!" hissed Vickery. "Save that line for the judge! Here—stick out your hands! There—now we're all set! Come along!"

Still dazed, I followed Hawkins down the steps, plucking at his arm as Vickery thrust his handcuffed captive with a rough shove into the rear seat of the sedan.

"For God's sake, what have you got on Karl?" I asked.

"The will," said Hawkins mysteriously.

"The will?" I parroted.

"Plenty of motive there, young fellow. Didn't know that, did you? I told 'em all to keep their mouths shut when they came back up here—I didn't want him to get suspicious before I got around to make the pinch. Of course, I didn't know about the note then—"

"So you know about the note, too?"

"Sure. I've just been talking with them over at the Inn. Nobody seems to have any idea how he happened to do it—"

"How who happened to do what?" I snapped in exasperation.

"How old Fitch happened to will that butler of his a hundred thousand dollars!" retorted Hawkins.

"*What?*"

The solicitor nodded portentously.

"New will made three days ago," he amplified. "No question but what he had some sort of a hold over his boss—scared him into it or something. And then he killed him—"

Sheriff Vickery jabbed the horn impatiently. I sought wildly for something further to say.

"So those other two didn't have anything to do with it?" I got out.

Hawkins, backing away, shook his head.

"I wasn't in favor of getting 'em back here in the first place," he said, "but Larry, he insisted on it. Of course, now that I'm in charge, I've turned 'em loose—"

"You've—you've turned them loose?" I faltered, horrified.

"Sure. Why not?"

My brain, stunned by the impact of the repeated hammerings it had just sustained, could at the moment produce no valid objection.

"But what about the note?" I managed feebly.

Hawkins, his foot on the running board, gave a scornful snort.

"Oh, he just wrote that himself to scare the rest off," he said.

I caught at his arm once more.

"Then he killed Guy Fitch and his wife too?" I demanded.

For the first time Hawkins displayed genuine doubt, and one hand strayed to his tortured sideburn.

"Well, it stands to reason," he said stubbornly, "'Course, I don't know just why—not so far, anyhow. But I'll sweat it out of him when I get him in jail!'"

I stood, tranced, staring after his car until its tail-light winked out of sight through the iron gates.

At the time I felt positive that Gene Hawkins had made some asinine error regarding the terms of old Peter's will. I was to learn later, however, that his information had been absolutely correct.

One hundred thousand dollars to Karl Litzler!

I learned later, also, of the other bequests, all equally typical of Peter Fitch. An equal sum—one hundred thousand dollars—went to George and Margery Wold. I wondered why Hawkins did not consider them equally suspicious characters until I found that he also knew the tale of Wenty's parentage.

Two millions went unreservedly to his favorite, Patty. A like amount was placed in joint trust for his widow, Nellie Fitch, and her half-sister, Alice Lodge—on condition that they continue to live together! I could almost hear old Peter's cackling chuckle as he had included this stipulation.

The remaining personal bequests were equally generous—five thousand each to Della and Mary, ten thousand to myself (though I could not imagine why), and substantial sums to a wide range of charities and individuals. The residue of the estate, through a typical Fitchian kink, had been left as an endowment for some theological school with which he had never in his life had the slightest connection.

But at the time I knew nothing of all these; I knew only of the butler's astounding windfall. And at the time, I admit, I saw far more warrant for Hawkins' arrest of Karl, than for Peter Fitch's lavish bequest to a mere servant, albeit a faithful and devoted one.

Despite the heat a sudden shiver passed up my spine as I realized that Karl's enforced departure left me alone on the mountain top with George and Margery. A fine pair, indeed, with which to spend the night at the scene where, within the past seventy-two hours, three brutal torch murders had been committed!

Dusk had already descended, and the shadows gathering about me looked sinister and menacing. I turned toward the house, to find it in total darkness.

For the moment I entertained the unpleasant notion that the Wolds likewise had vanished, leaving me in sole possession of Fitch's Folly.

Hastily I mounted the steps and passed through the lower floor, turning on the lights as I went. Their cheery brilliance made doubly disturbing the thought of my isolated room above the dark garage. I was already dead for sleep—had, in fact, been so for hours—and my nerves were literally twitching with fatigue. But I had no intention of retiring as long as I could possibly remain awake.

Hearing a slight noise behind the door of the Wolds' room as I passed, I paused and tapped on the panel.

"That you, Bill?" came a quavering voice.

"Yes. What are you doing?"

"I've gone to bed," came George's gloomy answer. "Locked my door, too. Say—Bill?"

"Yes?"

"I don't like this a little bit. Believe me, I'd be down in Vershire right now if it wa'n't for that wife of mine."

"Has she gone to bed, too?" I asked on a sudden impulse.

"Yes," said George after a perceptible pause. "Why?"

"Oh, nothing," I said carelessly. "I'm going to turn in pretty soon myself. Want me to lock up?"

"Lock up?" repeated George in obvious mystification. "That's Karl's job, ain't it?"

I had not realized that Karl's arrest and removal had been conducted so expeditiously as to pass unnoted. Briefly I explained what had occurred.

George, who did not sound in the least sleepy, swore in astonishment.

"Well, what do you know?" he said, his gloomy tones displaying marked relief. "Guess we'll all sleep better tonight, eh? No, never mind the doors, Bill. I'll get up and tend to 'em myself."

On tiptoe I let myself out into the darkness. With caution I circled the house, gun and flashlight ready, straining my eyes and ears into the gloom. For all George's optimism, I could not rid myself of the feeling that danger and death still stalked abroad on the mountain top.

Finding nothing amiss, I made my way to the garage, crept up the stairs to my room, and swept every corner with the beams of my torch before I left the threshold. But its rays revealed no hidden assassin lurking within, and I slumped into my easy chair, feeling more than a little foolish.

I had intended, after I had rested a moment and smoked a cigarette, to ring Larry and tell him of Karl's arrest. But the moment I relaxed my pent-up fatigue overwhelmed me. I inhaled deeply, hoping to keep awake, but my lids drooped despite my best efforts.

My last recollection was of drowsily stubbing out my half-burned cigarette and of telling myself that in another moment I would rise and walk myself back into wakefulness . . .

Somewhere a bell was ringing. It seemed to be a telephone bell. Sitting dizzily erect in the darkness, I thrust my hand out blindly toward the table by the window, sending the instrument crashing to the floor.

And as I stooped to pick it up, a voice sounded almost in my ear—a hideous, croaking voice, utterly unrecognizable.

"Water! For God's sake—Litzler?"

CHAPTER XVIII
NIGHTMARE

The words, to my fuddled senses, seemed to have come from the receiver. My skin crawled as I fumbled frantically about on the floor in the darkness. It seemed ages before my fingers finally closed about the phone.

Snatching it up, I held the mouthpiece to my lips.

"Hello?" I gasped.

There was no reply, and in the next instant the line went suddenly dead.

I might almost have imagined that I had dreamed the whole thing if I had not heard, before I was cut off, the faint, almost imperceptible sound of human breathing!

"Hello!" I cried. "Hello! Who is it?"

Dead silence was my only answer. But I was positive—unless the call had come from outside—that someone had been trying to use the intercommunicating telephone system at Fitch's Folly.

To eliminate the possibility of an outside call, I threw over the switch and jiggled the hook. I began to think the line had been cut before the sleepy voice of Steve Jacobson, night operator at the Vershire exchange, said thickly:

"Nummapleez?"

"Listen!" I said. "Did you put through an outside call for the Fitch place just now?"

"Zno one onna linowlya pleezexcusit," mumbled Jacobson, and I heard the click of the switchboard plug as he disconnected.

Convinced now that the call was of local origin, I switched on my lights, caught up my torch and revolver, and dashed down the stairs, trying as I ran to remember the location of the phones at Fitch's Folly.

There was one in the library, one in the lower hall, one in the butler's pantry, one in the upper hall, and one in Peter Fitch's former room on the northwest corner of the second floor. There had been one, I recalled, in the barn, now burned—besides, of course, my own in the garage.

From which of these had the mysterious call emanated?

Now fully awake after my brief nap, I hurried across the drive and lawn and circled the house once more, eyeing the windows searchingly. But my scrutiny revealed no gleam of light within; the huge edifice was in total darkness.

I halted irresolutely beneath the porte-cochère, in two minds whether to make a thorough search of the house or to set the whole thing down as either a delusion or a nightmare. And as I stood there, hesitating, I recalled something which I had all but forgotten.

There had been another phone—at the gardener's cottage!

There was still, in fact; for I now remembered that Larry had used it to summon Doc Reefer two nights earlier, when Martha Fitch had been found murdered there.

Turning, I crept cautiously toward the brow of the slope, within view of the half-burned structure below. Here, flattening myself out on the dewy grass, I lay motionless, staring with all my eyes.

For some moments, as I watched, all was dark and silent. I had all but started to rise when a light flickered suddenly through one of the casements, revealing a shadowy shape moving within.

Springing to my feet, I went pounding down the slope on the dead run, gun and torch tightly gripped in either hand. I was within thirty feet of the cottage when a whiter gleam against the blackness caught my eye, and I leveled my light at it with a thrill of triumph.

The beam fell full on the face of Margery Wold, clad in white, standing in the doorway. Her wild black eyes blinked shut as the light caught them, and her hand flew up in an involuntary shield. "Who is it?" she cried out harshly, a catch of fear in her voice. "What do you want?"

I stopped dead, feeling incredibly foolish.

"It's me—Bill Perley," I stammered awkwardly. "What on earth are you doing down here at this time of night?"

Margery, moving forward, seated herself on the steps as placidly as if such nocturnal prowls were her nightly custom—as, for all I knew, they might have been.

"I couldn't sleep," she said simply.

"Was that you I saw inside the cottage just now?" I demanded.

"Yes."

"What were you doing?"

"I remembered some jewelry I'd left down here. I've been lying awake, and I happened to think of it, so I came down to get it."

Her black eyes peered out at me stormily. "Satisfied?" she snapped.

Admittedly I was not, though I could not have told why. For a moment I debated forcing my way past her and making a search of the cottage. I have always wondered why I did not.

"Have you—has anyone been using the phone here?" I persisted, still keeping my torch focused on her face.

Her features, half hidden by her shielding hand, revealed a genuine bewilderment.

"This phone?" she said blankly. "I didn't even know it would work."

I stood irresolute, staring at her. Should I tell her of the croaking voice I had just heard, or would it create causeless alarm?

"Where's George?" I inquired at length. Scorn settled upon her sullen face.

"George?" she repeated, her voice edged with venom. "Asleep, I suppose—the poor coward! I heard him lock himself in after I went out! He'd be afraid to come out here like this tonight if he had the whole police force for a bodyguard!"

I cast about for an excuse to prolong the interview with this stolid, self-possessed woman seated as calmly on the steps of her former home as if utterly ignorant of the flaming terror which had walked abroad by night.

"And you're not afraid?" I asked finally.

Margery's black eyes lit with an eerie light. She rose to her feet, raising her arms skyward, her white-clad figure clear-cut against the charred wall behind her.

"Afraid?" she repeated. "Not Margery Wold! She's not afraid of God, man, nor devil!"

And with that she lifted her voice in a high-pitched laugh so wild, so shrill, so wholly horrible that it seemed to echo out across the sleeping valley like the laughter of the damned.

I am not ashamed to admit that it took real courage to turn my back upon those blazing eyes and ascend once more the slope leading up to the house. Behind the maniacal laughter died down, to be succeeded by an evil gurgle of merriment, low-pitched, bubbling in the madwoman's throat like the vile brew of a witch's caldron, which followed me until I was out of sight of the cottage.

Once more I circled the house, finding courage and curiosity alike oozing from my pores. Drugged with weariness, I found my feet moving mechanically, like those of a somnambulist. The whole affair, in fact, was beginning to assume the fantastic proportions of a nightmare.

Suddenly, as I neared the garage, I came wide awake in a flash. For I had seen, a lighter blur against the dark, a shadowy shape slip stealthily across my path.

Noiselessly I took up the pursuit, straining every sense to overtake the intruder without being myself observed, overwhelmingly determined to capture the flitting figure and settle once and for all the identity of the Fitch's Folly murderer.

Sprinting across the greensward on tiptoe, I tried to leap the drive in the darkness. My foot struck its far edge and slipped, sending me sprawling with a clatter of gravel which shattered the stillness irreparably.

I was up again in an instant, only to see my quarry veer sharply away from the house and head for the woods at top speed.

My flashlight had flown from my hand as I fell. Clawing it up, I darted in pursuit, leveling it as I ran. Its bobbing beam illuminated a flitting figure leaping desperately down the slope, its arms held awkwardly before it.

Tugging out my revolver, I halted to take aim; then, reconsidering, ran forward again. The fugitive, thanks to a head start, was already so far away that accurate aim at such a moving target was next to impossible. And besides, I preferred to capture the killer alive.

I soon found, however, that in our mad footrace down the sloping grounds the flitting figure before me was nearly my equal in speed, and that hours spent behind the wheel of a costly car have little actual training value for cross-country man-hunting.

The distance from the house to the wall was roughly, I should say, a half mile. And though I had succeeded in closing the gap in some measure, my quarry was still the better part of a hundred yards ahead as he shot over the wall and out of sight into the wooded forest below.

When, gasping like a stricken fish, I gained the outer boundary of the estate, the mysterious prowler was nowhere visible.

Panting, I leaned against the breast-high wall of crumbling stone, squirting the beam of my torch in every direction and striving without success to suppress the asthmatic sounds emanating from my bellows-like chest.

Save for my own breathing, I could hear no slightest sound.

It seemed impossible that the fugitive, crashing downward through the underbrush, was already out of earshot. Had he darted sidewise into the road, only a few rods distant, muffling his retreating footfalls in the soft dirt of its spongy surface? Or was he hiding almost within arm's reach, waiting to pounce upon me from behind should I press my search beyond the confines of the estate?

I stood wrestling angrily with the problem. It would be, I knew, almost impossible to find anyone in the pitch-black forest before me, and I had no desire to get a knife or a bullet in the back. On the other hand, it was doubly maddening to have had my hands almost upon my quarry, only to let him thus tamely escape.

In the end, permitting my common sense to triumph over my rash impulses, I reluctantly relinquished the pursuit and turned back once more toward the house. I was able at any rate to solace myself with the thought that I had probably scared the unknown out of a year's growth, and that his return that night to Fitch's Folly was extremely unlikely.

Still breathing heavily, I stumbled back up the slope toward the huge house, topped by its never-failing light. I was furiously angry at myself for having permitted the fugitive to escape; I might at least, I told myself, have taken a pot shot at him.

But shortly, as my wrath cooled, I found myself face to face with yet another problem—the true identity of the unknown prowler.

Had I not, a few hours earlier, seen Karl Litzler safely removed to jail, I would have sworn that he had been the nocturnal visitor. I had not seen his face at all, and his figure only in glimpses, but the general effect had been highly convincing. Or was Karl's image so firmly impressed on my mind that I had fallen victim to mental or optical illusion?

But if not Karl—who?

Was Wenty, despite the search, still running wild somewhere on the mountain? Had Dinwiddie reappeared in disguise on an errand utterly unfathomable? Had Smith or Robinson, now released, returned to Fitch's Folly? Had some prying reporter, sneaking in for a flashlight, fled carrying his camera before my pursuit? Or was some member of the party at the Inn—a woman, even, in masculine garb—slipping back into the grounds for the commission of a fresh crime?

I found myself standing stupidly before the porte-cochère, my head aching dully, my eyelids burning like fire, and my brain incapable of constructive thinking of any sort.

I had previously considered making a final search of the house before retiring, but in view of recent events this seemed rather pointless. Besides, I doubted if the terrified George, doubtless secure behind a newly-locked door, would have courage to admit me.

Now, standing there, I began to share and to appreciate his feelings. Discovery of the nocturnal prowler had shaken my nerves sadly; the darkness all about me seemed peopled with myriads of creeping, menacing figures.

Almost I regretted that I had obeyed the impulse to remain that night at Fitch's Folly. What could I do alone against the crafty killer who had baffled all efforts to bring him to book?

If Larry were only with me . . .

With a start I realized that I was all but asleep on my feet. Unless I was to drop in my tracks, it was imperative that I snatch at least a few hours' rest.

Propping my burning lids ajar, I dragged my weary frame stiffly back to the garage, up the stairs, and into my room. Locking the door securely behind me, I thrust a chair beneath the knob, snapped off the light, staggered across to my bed, and threw myself, fully dressed, upon it.

. . . The fire nightmare again. The acrid odor of smoke in my cringing nostrils. The crackling flames outside, their dread approach holding me tranced, spellbound, able only to lie quaking in nameless terror.

I tried to awaken, for I knew, subconsciously, that it was only a dream. I strove to move, but was powerless.

Someone, far off, was calling my name. I shrieked an answer, but my stiff lips made no sound.

I dreamed that I awoke—but even then the nightmare of fire persisted. Then, with startling suddenness, I was awake—and it was no nightmare, but hideous reality!

The garage was afire. Sheets of flame soared hissing past my window, revealing serpents of smoke seeping through the cracks of the floor. I lay frozen with fear, staring in horrible fascination.

From bad dreams there was at long last, however tardy, a merciful awakening. But from grim reality—

A tongue of flame licked at the window beside my bed. The glass cracked and fell inward, and the scarlet tongue crept hungrily toward me.

Dimly, as my senses left me, I heard the pounding of feet on the stairs and a heavy hand hammering at my door. I had fainted dead away from fright when the panels burst inward and strong arms, lifting my unconscious form, bore me from the blazing building.

CHAPTER XIX
SMOKE AND FLAME

I awoke on a high, narrow bed of iron, with narrow white walls pressing in upon me. I struggled up with a hoarse cry, the vivid vision of smoke and flame still etched on my eyeballs.

Then, as my mind cleared, I saw with a shock that I was in one of the private rooms of the Vershire General Hospital.

A white-clad nurse, rising from her chair, picked up a glass from the bedside table.

"You're all right, Mr. Perley," she said soothingly. "Just drink this and go back to sleep."

"But—"

"Everything's all right. Now be a good fellow and drink this."

I obeyed reluctantly, my head buzzing with a million questions. But shortly, as the sedative took effect, my anxieties became inconsequential, and, closing my eyes, I drifted away into dreamless slumber.

When I awoke once more the sunlight was streaming in at my westward window. Immeasurably refreshed, I turned my head on my pillow.

In the chair beside my bed sprawled a lanky figure, black eyes fixed searchingly on my face.

"Larry!" I cried joyfully.

"Yours truly, Bill. How goes it?"

"Better," I said, wrinkling my forehead. "How did I get here?"

"I brought you," grinned Larry. "Don't you remember?"

"Then it was you—hammering at the door?" I cried. "It was you that saved my life?"

Larry squirmed and looked sheepish.

"But what were you doing up at Fitch's Folly?" I persisted. "I thought you'd been taken off the case?"

"I have—officially. But you didn't think I was going to quit, did you?"

"But Gene Hawkins—"

"To hell with Gene Hawkins and Nellie Fitch and all the rest of them!" flared Larry. "I started this, and, by God, I'm going to finish it!"

He stopped, looking a little shamefaced, and his face cracked into a grin.

"I'm doing this on my own," he explained. "Larry Frost—private detective. That's why I was up on the mountain last night. Lucky for you, too, I guess. You'd passed out cold before I smashed in the door—"

I felt the muscles of my cheeks stiffen at the ghastly memory thus conjured up.

"Did you see—who did it?" I asked him in a low tone.

Larry shook his dark head.

"I was up on the ridge, the other side of the house, when I saw the fire," he said. "I wasn't expecting anything like that, and I can't figure out yet how it happened. What made you stay up there last night, anyhow?"

He listened intently as I outlined the night's activities at Fitch's Folly. Before I had finished, he had risen and was striding to and fro excitedly.

"That clinches it!" he exclaimed, his black eyes burning. "If I can find out one thing more—"

"What clinches it?" I queried blankly.

"What you've just told me."

"But I didn't tell you anything," I protested.

"That's what you think," retorted Larry cryptically. "Of course, there's always the chance that I'm wrong, you know. But if I'm right—and I think I am—I'm going to put on a real show tonight!"

"What sort of a show?"

Larry, pausing by the bed, laid a soothing hand on my arm.

"Nothing you're going to get in on, Bill," he said firmly. "You lie right here and take it easy—I'll be in and see you again before night.

Right now I've got a million things to do, and I can't waste time hanging around any invalids!"

Flashing a grin over his shoulder, he departed precipitately, leaving my brain surging with unspoken questions.

I divided the remainder of the afternoon between trying to marshal them into some semblance of order and pleading unsuccessfully for permission to get up and dress. I still felt decidedly weak and shaky, but if further excitement was due that night I had no intention of missing it.

The nurse had just removed my supper tray when he returned, his lanky frame fairly radiating vigor and enthusiasm. At my first salvo of questions he lifted a protesting hand.

"Take it easy, Bill," he said, lowering himself into the chair beside my bed. "I'm not going to tell you all I know—yet. Time enough later, if things work out as I'm planning.

"I will tell you this much, though. This whole affair is cut from the same piece of cloth. It started the morning of the day before the Fourth—the day Dinwiddie came—and it was due to end night before last. The burning of the garage was an afterthought—"

"Have you found out who Dinwiddie was?" I broke in.

Larry nodded slowly.

"Yes," he admitted. "But I'm not going to tell you now—except that Dinwiddie is an alias. It's not his real name at all."

"How do you mean?"

"He came here under an assumed name. And he came in disguise—if you can call removing a toupee a disguise. Actually, he's as bald as an egg, though you'd never guess it from that picture."

"But why did he come to Fitch's Folly?"

"For money," said Larry, and would not amplify his statement.

"Then you don't think Brown and Robinson were mixed up in it after all?" I asked, taking a new tack.

"I didn't say that, Bill. But if my theory is right, they were no part of the original plan—they merely happened along to make it harder."

He sat silent for a moment, drumming rhythmically on the arms of his rocker.

"Another loose end I've cleaned up," he said, "is the bullet. The report of the ballistics expert didn't help much—he couldn't tell

whether the cartridge was exploded by rim fire or center fire without
having the shell. But all the same, I'm positive now that it was from
Peter Fitch's gun and not from George Wold's."

"Why?"

"Tell you later, Bill—after the big show. Anything else?"

My thoughts floundered clumsily among the tangled threads of
the case.

"Who sent Nellie Fitch that telegram?" I asked.

Larry's black eyes gleamed mischievously.

"I did," he admitted.

"You?"

"Sure. I fixed it with the telegraph operator. He's a good egg,
too—lied himself black in the face for me. Old Nellie's still raising
heaven and earth to trace it, but I'm afraid she's out of luck. She's
doubly suspicious, of course, because I slipped up on the spelling of
the name I signed."

I closed my mouth, which had fallen ajar, and lay regarding Larry
in blank amazement.

"What on earth did you do it for?" I asked.

The gleam of amusement died abruptly in Larry's eyes.

"Because I miscalculated," he answered grimly. "I'd figured she
was slated to go next, rather than old Peter—and I figured the safest
thing was to have her called to New York. At that, I may have saved
her life. I don't know."

Uncoiling his long legs, he rose to his feet and stood staring at the
late summer sunlight outside.

"There are a lot of other things I don't know, too," he said mus-
ingly. "But with good luck I'll have the answer to most of them tonight. Now you keep on staying right where you are, and don't get
any crazy idea of trying to get up and help me. I'm still bucking Gene
and Oscar, but I can make the grade just the same."

"But, Larry—" I protested wildly.

Larry, shaking his head, laid a kindly hand on my shoulder.

"You had too damned close a call last night, Bill, to take any more
chances," he said. "You're not in such good shape as you think you
are—those fires and lack of sleep together have raised hell with your
nerves. Tomorrow morning's plenty of time to get up."

"But—"

"I'll leave you the Vershire *Journal-Transcript* to amuse you. If you don't run a fever over Gene's yarn in there, you're beyond hope. I blew out a couple of fuses myself—and I only read half of it at that."

I lay listening to his retreating footsteps, privately determined to participate in the grand finale that night, hospital or no hospital. In the meantime, picking up the afternoon paper he had tossed on the bed, I soon learned what had sent Larry's temperature soaring.

The slow-moving Drago county solicitor, suddenly elevated to a position of national importance in the eyes of press and public, had abandoned himself without restraint to the intoxication of publicity. "Solicitor Hawkins says" occurred in nearly every line of the bold-faced type beneath the even blacker streamer spread across the top of the page. Fascinated, I read:

> "Convinced beyond the shadow of a doubt that he has the murderer of Fitch's Folly under lock and key, County Solicitor Eugene V. Hawkins today renewed his grilling of Karl Litzler, butler and valet at the summer home of Peter Fitch, Albany millionaire, held without bail for the series of brutal torch murders culminating forty-eight hours ago in the slaying of his employer and the burning of his body beneath the windmill.
>
> "Despite the fact that Litzler, whom County Sheriff Oscar Vickery took into custody last night after a desperate struggle and who was later recaptured in a state of collapse just outside the grounds following a break for liberty en route to jail—"

(So it had been Karl that I chased, after all!)

> "—has so far failed to weaken under the merciless cross-questioning to which he has been subjected, Solicitor Hawkins feels confident that his ultimate breakdown and confession is imminent. The mass of evidence against him, Solicitor Hawkins says, is sufficiently conclusive in itself to send the slayer to the

chair, but he is certain that before many hours Litzler will tell all.

"Already, Solicitor Hawkins says, Litzler has admitted setting fire to the woods at the rear of Fitch's Folly on the night of Peter Fitch's murder, although he steadfastly refuses to give his reasons for this act. Unquestionably, Solicitor Hawkins says, this was done to attract the attention of guards and to create a diversion under cover of which he was able to return, murder his employer, drag his body to the mill, and there ignite the structure. Somehow, Solicitor Hawkins says, he had gained knowledge of the $100,000 legacy contained in Peter Fitch's will, and avarice and cupidity had done the rest.

"The occupants of the mountain estate, who spent the night at the Vershire Inn as the result of a death threat note presumably planted by Litzler to insure their absence while he made his getaway, returned to Fitch's Folly today after Solicitor Hawkins had assured them that the murders had been solved and that the murderer was in custody.

"Last night's fire at Fitch's Folly, in which William Perley, chauffeur, narrowly escaped being burned to death, had no connection whatsoever with the series of torch slayings, Solicitor Hawkins stated positively today. He advanced the theory that Perley had probably fallen asleep while holding a lighted cigarette, and that this had ignited the garage, from which the chauffeur was carried unconscious.

"Perley, who Solicitor Hawkins says was at one time seriously considered as a suspect owing to peculiar actions reported by the widow of the murdered man when he was seen trying to hide himself in the cupola, is now in a critical condition at the Vershire General Hospital—"

Angrily I rent the news print asunder and with twitching fingers pressed the buzzer vigorously.

"I want to get up!" I announced when the nurse appeared.

Smiling, she shook her head.

"Sorry, Mr. Perley. You're to stay here until tomorrow. Doctor's orders."

"Damn the doctor and his orders! I've got to get out of here to-night!"

"That's impossible, Mr. Perley. I'm sorry! Tomorrow—"

"Let me see the superintendent!" I demanded.

But the superintendent, a huge, impervious mountain of a woman, turned a deaf ear to my frantic demands.

"I should say not!" she said with grim decision. "I am responsible to Doctor Reefer for your condition, and I shall certainly not give consent to your release without his permission!"

At length, urgently importuned, she departd grudgingly to call Doc Reefer. His point-blank refusal, of which with immense satisfaction she shortly informed me, served to crystallize my conviction that Larry Frost was solely responsible for my detention.

Fuming but impotent, I settled myself with as good grace as possible to pass the dragging hours which must intervene before my release. But as dusk settled down over the valley, I grew increasingly restless. Before the night nurse had switched off my light at eight o'clock, I was in a state of impatience bordering on distraction.

My thoughts, I need not state, centered upon Ruth Vale, who had been much in my mind during the day. If the Vershire *Journal-Transcript* was correct, she had returned to Fitch's Folly to spend the night. And if, as Larry had hinted, the last act of the tragic drama was still to be played—who knew into what fresh danger she might have unwittingly ventured?

I have never been a believer in premonitions, and I am still, I confess, a skeptic. But as I lay there I found myself becoming completely obsessed with the conviction that Ruth was in deadly peril, and that my place was at Fitch's Folly.

Sitting upright, I peered through the westward window. The sun had long since set, but the sky above the mountain top still showed a trace of pure gold. On such a night, I recalled, and with such a sun-set, I had emerged into the street to see tiny tongues of flame licking skyward.

I sat erect with a start. Did my eyes deceive me, or did they discern a flicker of fire?

But after a moment I relaxed, to lie sweating and shivering between the sticky sheets. It had been merely the faint gleam of light in the cupola, a bare pinpoint against the enshrouding darkness.

My nerves by now had taken full possession of me. I tried to woo slumber, but without success. The moments dragged interminably as I lay there tense, helpless, my fears mounting, my enforced inaction growing steadily more unendurable.

It was well on toward midnight when at last, with defiance born of desperation, I slipped stealthily out of bed and tiptoed to the cabinet in the corner, where I found, as I had hoped, my clothes. Shakily I donned them in the darkness, my ears alert for the approach of the night supervisor on her rounds. I was well aware that the superintendent, her authority defied, would not hesitate to put me in a strait-jacket if necessary should she find me in the act of escaping.

I had just finished dressing when I heard footsteps in the corridor outside. I shrank back into the corner, praying that they might pass. Instead, they halted opposite my door, and I heard a soft but startled gasp which indicated that my empty bed had been noted.

Darting to the open window, I peered out into the darkness. By good fortune I had been placed on the ground floor. Wriggling over the sill, I managed to drop from sight just as the light flashed on in my room and a sharp cry shrilled in my ears.

I broke into a feverish run, heading for the nearest taxi stand. It was only four blocks away, but I was panting with nervousness and exhaustion before I reached it.

Two night cabs stood at the curb, their drivers smoking nearby. The pair wheeled, startled, as I sprang into the nearest machine.

"Fitch's Folly—and make it snappy!" I gasped.

"Up on the mountain?" yawned the driver, clambering in behind the wheel.

"Yes! Get going, will you?"

The cab lurched into motion. I sat on the edge of the seat, my hands clenching and unclenching. Our progress seemed maddeningly slow. I found myself muttering impatient curses beneath my breath as the machine careened roaring up the slope of the mountain.

What if Larry's plans—whatever they were—had gone astray? What if the torch slayer had reappeared at Fitch's Folly for a final fling? What if Ruth—

The cab, flashing through the open gates, shot out of the ring of woods. I leaned forward, peering through the windshield as we lurched crazily up the sloping drive.

The next instant my bones turned to water, and chill fingers of fear plucked at the pit of my stomach.

The glare of flames shone redly through the windows of the big house, half obscured by billowing clouds of black smoke. A shrill scream rang in my ears as I swu.4ng out onto the running board, clinging there desperately as the cab skidded to a stop.

There were running figures all about me in the darkness, but to these I paid no heed. I had eyes only for the window almost directly above my head.

Framed in the casement stood Ruth, her white arms outstretched imploringly, her slender body silhouetted against the red glare within!

CHAPTER XX
FINIS!

I have never been able to fathom the source whence I derived the insane, unthinking courage for my mad dash into the smoke-filled building—an act which, incidentally, served to shatter once and for all my fire phobia. Frankly, I did not even stop to think of the danger, or of my fear; my only thought was of Ruth, trapped and helpless in the chamber above.

Someone grabbed my arm as I leaped up the steps. It was Larry.

"Wait a minute, Bill!" he yelled. "It isn't—"

Wrenching away, I filled my lungs and plunged blindly through the doorway.

The billowing smoke was stifling as I groped my way up the staircase, and glare of lurid crimson half blinded me as I reached the upper hall. But the floor beneath my feet was still solid as, shielding my eyes, I burst into the room—strangling, choking, half suffocated, my eyeballs smarting intolerably.

Ruth turned from the open window. I shall never forget the look in her bright dark eyes as she recognized me.

"Bill!" she cried incredulously.

I reached her side in time to catch her as she slumped limply. Holding her in my arms, I dragged her to the casement. Behind us the lurid flames glared redly, and the black smoke, billowing past us in stifling clouds, made breathing possible only spasmodically.

As I gathered myself for the dash back down the staircase, I heard my name called from the ground below, and the top of a ladder smacked against the woodwork almost level with the sill.

"Bill!" came Larry's voice.

"Yes?" I choked.

"Come on down! Use the ladder!"

My head was whirling as I clambered awkwardly over the sill and lifted Ruth's unconscious form through the window after me. Vertigo assailed me as I fumbled for the rungs beneath my feet. It seemed ages before I felt firm ground.

For a moment I stood upright, avidly filling my wheezing lungs with the fresh night air. Then, as someone relieved me of my burden, I pitched forward and lay prone, stricken with violent nausea.

I felt myself lifted to my feet.

"Who said you were afraid of fire?" Larry muttered in my ear.

"I had to get her out," I coughed weakly.

"Why didn't you stay in the hospital where you belonged? So help me God, I'll half kill that bunch for letting you in on this! If I'd ever dreamed— Didn't you know when I tried to stop you?"

I wheeled on him angrily.

"I suppose you'd have let her stay in there and burn to death!" I snarled. "If I hadn't come—"

"Burn to death?" repeated Larry. "She wouldn't burn— Wait a minute! I've been so busy with you I clean forgot—"

He wheeled and darted away into the darkness. Bewildered, I stumbled feebly after him, clutching his arm as he halted perhaps thirty feet away.

"What do you mean, 'She wouldn't burn'?" I demanded.

Larry stood rooted to the spot, staring upward at the dark facade of Fitch's Folly.

"I'm sorry about all this, Bill," he said quietly. "You see, there's no fire!"

I blinked stupidly, uncomprehending. Surely this was all part of another nightmare!

"No fire?" I parroted, waving a flaccid arm toward the red-lit casements. "Then what—"

"Red fire and smoke bombs, Bill—to smoke out the rats. I rigged this up myself—"

His voice broke oddly as he twitched away. He pointed upward, his arm quivering.

"By God!" he said in a hushed voice. "There he is!"

My eyes followed the direction of his pointing arm. The next instant I found myself clinging to him dizzily—staring, aghast, incredulous.

Atop the sloping roof of Fitch's Folly one of the tiny windows of the octagonal cupola had been swung open. Through it was scrambling frantically a figure, tiny and black and somehow hideous against the yellow light within.

I shuddered as a cracked scream of pure terror echoed across the mountain top. I shall never forget that scream.

"Help! Fire! Help! Help!"

My temples throbbed as if they would burst; my dry tongue lolled foolishly between my stiff lips as I stared, stricken dumb with sheer shock.

For the voice and the figure were those of Peter Fitch!

The tiny black figure, still screaming, crawled clear of the cupola window and lay clinging precariously to the slippery slates. A cry burst from Larry's lips as it began to scramble its way desperately upward toward the ridgepole, only to slip and catch itself by one corner of the cupola.

"Hang on, Mr. Fitch!" he shouted. "It's all right! We'll get you down!"

At the sound of Larry's voice old Peter stiffened and lay still. Then, with a cry of utter despair, his hold loosened and he began to slide with increasing speed toward the edge of the roof.

As the body shot out over the edge of the eaves, my overtaxed nerves snapped under the strain and I pitched forward unconscious in a state of complete collapse. I did not hear nor see Peter Fitch's body strike the ground, to lie limp and crumpled upon the graveled drive. And I never knew—nor did Larry—whether his fall had been due to the shock of Larry's shout, or whether, realizing that he had been outwitted, he had deliberately chosen death.

I regained consciousness to find myself once more an inmate of the Vershire General Hospital, and Larry once more beside me. It was mid-morning, and the bright sunshine outside wove dancing patterns of leaves upon the white clapboards of the house across the street.

"Where's—Peter?" was my first feeble query.

"In the next room," replied Larry soberly.

"Alive?" I gasped.

"Not now. He died about a half hour ago. The undertaker's on his way here now."

He paused, staring somberly at the opposite wall.

"He talked—before he died," he said slowly. "Enough to hang him, too, for all his millions. Of course, he could probably have worked an insanity plea—high-priced alienists and all that. But he's better dead, and I guess he knew it."

"Larry!" I said after a moment.

"Yes, Bill?"

"Was he really crazy—demented, I mean?"

"Well, yes—and no. I'd say, rather, he was pitiless—the terrible ruthlessness of a rich old man who'd always had his own way and who intended to keep on having it at any cost. Erratic, eccentric—yes, I grant you that. But if I were on a jury I'd hold out till hell froze over before I'd call him insane.

"I'll admit he had a persecution complex, but that's not insanity. And he was obsessed by fires—loved 'em and hated 'em both—to such an extent that he might rate as an incipient pyromaniac. It's not so hard, looking back, to see why he hired you. In some ways you two aren't so different after all.

"But when he let himself go, it was deliberately and with malice aforethought. Judging by the way he's talked, he'd had it on his mind for months. You can't tell me different. I've been listening to him. I know."

I struggled to sit upright, then sank back again. "But did he really kill Guy and Martha—and try to kill me?" I asked.

"Yes, Bill."

"But why? For God's sake, why?"

Larry, glancing over his shoulder at the open door, lowered his voice and edged his chair nearer my bed.

"It started when Guy brought Dinwiddie to Fitch's Folly the day before the Fourth," he began. "I told you his real name wasn't Dinwiddie. I traced him down through the photographer. He was Dr. Thaddeus Rush, one of New York's lesser known alienists. As it happened, he sailed the following day for Europe. I doubt if he's heard, even yet, of the murders. Certainly he hasn't communicated with us.

"Guy resented old Peter's rule, his crack-brained antics, his tight hold on the family purse-strings. He arranged to have Dinwiddie—Rush, I mean—come up incognito ostensibly as a business guest and look old Peter over and see if he could be adjudged insane—at least sufficiently insane to have a conservator appointed. Of course, there was nothing unethical about that—from Dinwiddie's standpoint, I mean. But Guy knew that if old Peter suspected what he was up to, there'd be hell to pay. Hence the secrecy.

"Dinwiddie—I mean Rush—stopped at the barn—remember? He wanted a last word in private with Guy. Old Peter had been suspicious all day—that accounted for part of his crazy antics, like his stunt of talking outside the garage so you could overhear. He'd taken good care that Guy and the doctor shouldn't be alone together. He'd hidden himself in the barn before you stopped there, and he overheard enough to confirm his worst fears.

"You can talk all you want about brainstorms and temporary insanity and all the rest of the lingo. But I tell you that Peter Fitch was as sane as you or I when he slipped back to his room, loaded up his old revolver, came back and shot Guy through the head, stripped off his clothes, and touched a match to the hay.

"The fireworks downtown, of course, masked the sound of the shot. The gun and cartridges, he told me, he dropped in the disused well back of the barn—Hawkins and Vickery are looking for them now. He took Guy's clothes because he was clever enough to realize it would hamper identification. He buried them under the big pine while everyone was milling around the barn. He didn't know till I told him that Wenty'd seen him, but it wouldn't have worried him much, anyhow. In fact, one of his main ideas in getting Wenty freed was to have him handy for a scapegoat in case the scent got too hot."

"But where did Brown and Robinson fit?" I demanded. "Were they in on it somehow?"

Larry shook his head.

"They just walked into it, Bill," he said. "They'd been hanging around Vershire getting the lay of the land—somebody'd probably tipped them off to old Peter's vice of having stacks of real dough on hand. They simply sneaked in, trussed him up when he came down-stairs, looted the safe, and then beat it. The fire in the waste-basket was apparently just an accident—one of them probably dropped a butt in among the papers.

"That tickled the old man, too—gave him another scapegoat. I've broadcast another alarm for them, by the way—but shucks! What's robbery compared with three murders and an attempted fourth?"

"Three murders? But—"

"I'm coming to that, Bill. The second, of course, was Martha. Once she'd found out about Dinwiddie, he had to get rid of her before she could talk. She knew too much for old Peter's peace of mind, and too little to appreciate her own danger. It was easy for him to lure her down to the cottage on some pretext, smash her skull from be-hind, stuff her body into the closet, and later set the cottage afire. If Margery had been a sound sleeper, there might easily have been two more victims. But she woke up, and the shower came . . .

"Even then I hadn't suspected old Peter. There were too many false clues—Wenty's queerness, George's gun, the pair down at the inn, Gilbert's scrap with his future father-in-law, Ruth's mix-up with Guy—"

"Patty told you that?" I demanded incredulously.

"Oh, yes. Gilbert was something of hers, and she'd fight for him with every weapon she had. Ruth needn't know, of course—unless you think best to tell her. It wasn't malice on Patty's part, you know—just the Fitch blood cropping out."

I lay staring miserably at the ceiling. I could see Larry's view-point, and Patty's as well; but at the moment it seemed that I could never forgive old Peter's granddaughter.

"We come now to the third murder," resumed Larry. "And here, I'm willing to admit, Peter Fitch began to show definite symptoms of megalomania. The first two, in his own eyes, were justified—but his success in these had begun to go to his head. The third he planned to wind up the series in a blaze of glory and eliminate him from the pic-ture completely. Exactly how he planned to accomplish it, I haven't the remotest idea—"

"But who was the third victim?" I broke in. "It wasn't—it couldn't have been—Wenty?"

"No, Bill—it wasn't Wenty. Wenty has been roosting in his favorite hiding place—up in the thick branches of the big pine, completely concealed from the searchers. I corralled him quietly last evening and shipped him back to the State Hospital, where he belongs—I didn't want him mixed up in last night's affair. And this time he won't have his grandfather to help him get away."

"Then—that's why—"

"Exactly. That's why his folks looked so tickled, that day at the cottage. That's why Margery wouldn't leave. She'd been feeding him on the quiet. In fact, he was down at the cottage with her last night—you almost caught him. But he hid, and she bluffed you out of it."

"But the wax image?"

"What wax image?"

I told him of my find on Margery's bureau. He nodded slowly.

"That would be old Peter," he said. "Margery's always hated him, in spite of all he's done for them. She was probably trying to live up to her reputation for witchcraft. Maybe she actually believed in her own powers. She may have made it before the killings began, or after. It doesn't matter.

"But the third murder—"

I struggled up in bed once more.

"Yes?" I cried eagerly. "Who was it?"

"The tramp," said Larry.

"The tramp? You mean—"

"The tramp with the false teeth. Remember?"

I could almost feel my brain click as the picture fell into shape.

"Then he was the one—in the windmill shack?" I asked.

Larry nodded slowly.

"Yes—poor devil!" he said. "It was he, of course, who stole Guy's suit after Wenty dug it up. It was he who was wearing it when you saw him from your window. Peter Fitch had been giving him handouts—money and food—to keep him hanging around up there and sleeping in the woods. He thought he was playing old Peter for a good thing. If he'd ever realized—"

"But why didn't they find him when they searched the woods?"

"Because he wasn't there. He skipped out and left his hide-out when things began to get too hot for him—"

"But where did he go?"

"To Della Dole's."

"To Della Dole's?" I repeated weakly.

"He was her half-brother," Larry explained. "He'd hitch-hiked on from the West—she didn't even recognize him until he appealed to her for shelter. Naturally, she was ashamed to admit it, and a little worried, too. I've been having a talk with her this morning. By the way, she was the one that gave the alarm for the forest fire that night—the woman's voice we heard, you know."

"But—"

"Well, at any rate, old Peter killed him—lured him to the windmill shack by offering him more money. He left the body there all day— that's how nervy he was getting—and arranged for Karl to fire the woods that night to draw us all off. He'd also impressed on Karl that he must stay at Fitch's Folly at all costs. That explains the fight Karl put up to get away."

"Then Karl was equally guilty after all?"

Larry shook his head once more.

"Only of setting the forest fire," he said. "Karl was loyal, but dumb. He knew nothing of old Peter's plans to disappear. The old man had promised him a handsome reward, but Karl had no idea the money was to be left in the will. He merely obeyed orders blindly—and, as you know, later collapsed from nervous strain and shock.

"So while everyone was down in the woods—including those two dumb clucks of mine—old Peter headed for the windmill shack. He came on Ruth Vale in the upper hall and knocked her senseless. He soaked the tramp's body and the shack in kerosene after slipping into his mouth the set of teeth he'd had made in Vershire—the ones he was sure would be identified—and touched a match to it all.

"And then he pulled off the most childish, eccentric trick of all. He hid himself in the cupola!"

I started to speak, but Larry forestalled me.

"I didn't know," he went on rapidly, "until I'd questioned Nellie Fitch yesterday afternoon, that years ago the cupola was his favorite lookout. He'd had it fitted up with a rope ladder, an easy chair, a telescope, and even an extension phone. But lately it had been closed and locked and practically forgotten.

"He'd sneaked a stock of food and water up there—how and when, I don't know. And when he'd fired the shack he hurried back, climbed the stepladder, unlocked the trap door, let down the rope ladder, replaced the stepladder in the closet, climbed the rope ladder, and locked himself in.

"Just what he planned next, I don't know. I doubt if he did. Apparently he figured on slipping out the next night after dropping the death warning through the trap—the note the breeze carried down the upper hall to the head of the stairs. He may have planned to take Karl with him. He may have planned to kill Karl and leave a fake suicide note containing a confession. He wouldn't tell me that, and after all it doesn't matter.

"But at this point his luck turned. First of all, he upset his can of water—remember the spot on the ceiling you told me you thought was a leak in the roof after the shower? He suffered terribly from thirst—so terribly that he finally took a desperate chance and tried to get Karl on the phone. He didn't know, you see, that Karl had been arrested and taken away.

"When he heard your voice answer, he felt sure he had been discovered. Beside himself, he risked a final sally from his hiding place, refilled his can with water, and tried to burn down the garage.

"I'd been skeptical of those false teeth from the start—it's getting altogether too easy to establish false identities that way in arson cases. And after I'd found that 'Dinwiddie' was an alienist, the whole thing began to shape up in my mind. Your story of the phone call clinched it. I knew then that old Peter wasn't dead at all, and when his wife told me about the cupola, I felt certain that I knew where he was hiding."

He paused, brushing back his crisp hair with an abstracted hand. His dark face was hard and stern, and there was no trace of regret in his voice.

"I didn't suppose my fake fire would cause the old devil's death," he said. "I decided to stage it to give him a taste of what he'd been giving all the others—yourself included. I'm sorry about the scare I gave you—and the rest, too, of course—but I had to have genuine atmosphere to put it across."

He reared his lanky length from his chair, his black eyes glittering and merciless.

"But as far as Peter Fitch himself is concerned," he said harshly, "I haven't a regret in the world. I'd do it again tomorrow if I had the chance."

He shook himself abruptly, and the harsh lines of his face softened.

"Well, that's that," he said. "And I hadn't intended to take so much of your time, Bill. I almost forgot there was another visitor waiting to see you."

"Another visitor?" I repeated blankly.

Larry tiptoed to the door and beckoned. A moment later Ruth stood on the threshold.

She paused a moment, her bright dark eyes on mine. Then, crossing, she impulsively gave me both slim white hands.

"I won't stay but a minute, Bill," she said with adorable shyness. "I just wanted to thank you for—for last night and—and everything. And I'll see you again tomorrow. I know you need rest and quiet—"

For answer I tightened my hold on her slender wrists.

"Hang rest and quiet!" I said, a little breathlessly. "I know what I need!"

And as with flushed cheeks she bent above me, Larry, finger at lips and one eye significantly closed, softly pulled the door shut behind him.

COACHWHIP PUBLICATIONS
CoachwhipBooks.com

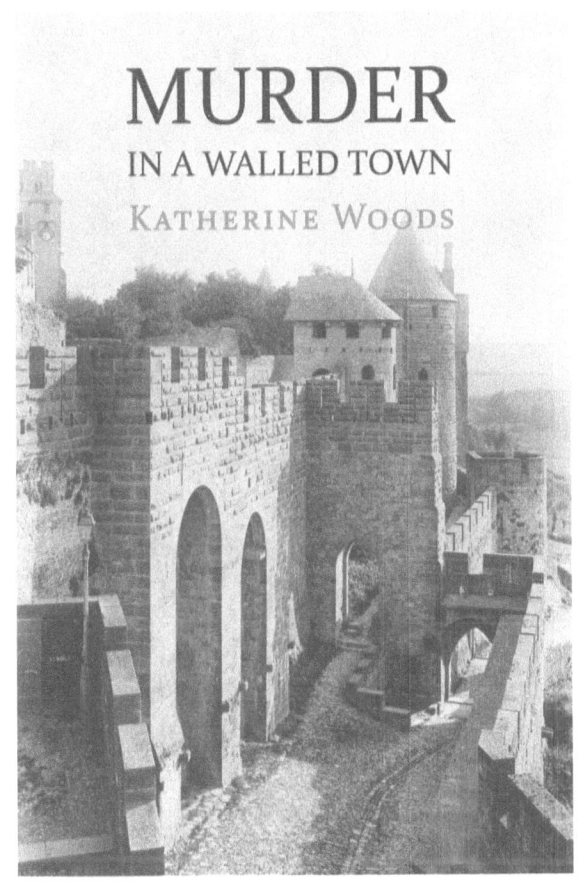

COACHWHIP PUBLICATIONS
CoachwhipBooks.com

COACHWHIP PUBLICATIONS
CoachwhipBooks.com

COACHWHIP PUBLICATIONS

CoachwhipBooks.com

**VULTURES
IN THE SKY**
A HUGH RENNERT MYSTERY

TODD DOWNING

COACHWHIP PUBLICATIONS
CoachwhipBooks.com

FULL CRASH DIVE

ALLAN R. BOSWORTH

COACHWHIP PUBLICATIONS
CoachwhipBooks.com

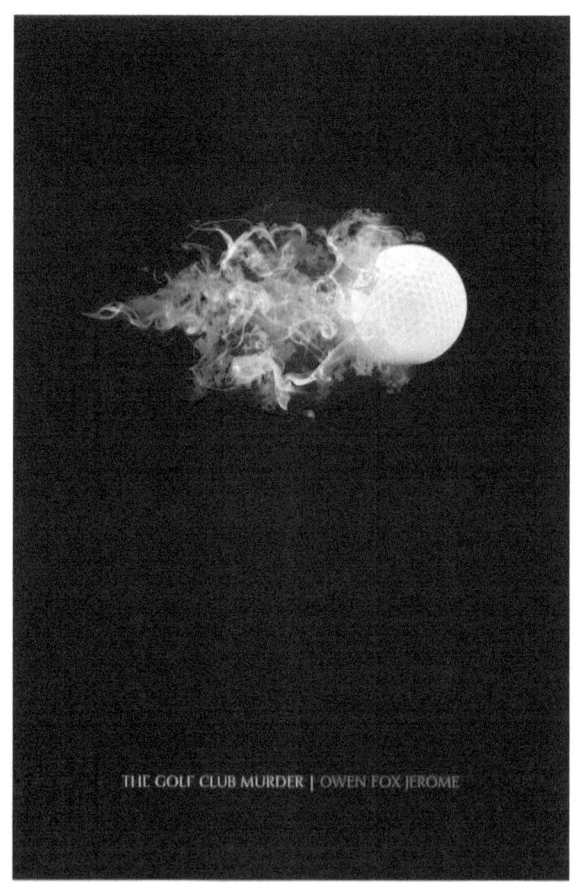

THE GOLF CLUB MURDER | OWEN FOX JEROME

COACHWHIP PUBLICATIONS
CoachwhipBooks.com

THE HEX MURDER

Alexander Williams

www.ingramcontent.com/pod-product-compliance
Lightning Source LLC
Chambersburg PA
CBHW020646260626
47157CB00008B/2921